Mia flinched. "You can dismiss your past commitment to me so easily?" Suddenly, she could scarcely breathe. "It meant so little to you?"

"It meant everything to me."

"Except for the part about you not coming with me." Mia closed the distance between them, the firmness of her strides sending her skirts swaying like wind-tossed treetops.

"You abandoned me. You made a promise—"

"Don't you talk to me about promises. You made a promise to me." She jabbed her finger into the center of his chest. "You said you'd love me forever." She poked him again. "You said you would honor and respect my wish to write. You—"

He clasped her jabbing finger in his hand. "I had no future in Boston. You wouldn't listen to me about that. You wanted your own way without listening to my side of things. And now, Mia, *mi amore...*" He closed his eyes and raised her hand to his cheek.

## LAURIE ALICE EAKES

"Eakes has a charming way of making her novels come to life without being over the top," writes *RT Book Reviews* of bestselling, award-winning author Laurie Alice Eakes. Since she lay in bed as a child telling herself adventure stories, she has fulfilled her dream of becoming a published author. With over a dozen books and novellas in print, she writes full-time from her home in Texas.

LAURIE ALICE EAKES

# The Professor's Heart

HEARTSONG
PRESENTS

Recycling programs
for this product may
not exist in your area.

LOVE INSPIRED BOOKS

ISBN-13: 978-0-373-48685-4

THE PROFESSOR'S HEART

www.Harlequin.com

**Printed in U.S.A.**

No servant can serve two masters:
for either he will hate the one, and love the other;
or else he will hold to the one, and despise the
other. Ye cannot serve God and mammon.
—*Luke* 16:13

To Gina, Patty and Pamela—How blessed I am to have worked with the three of you.

# Chapter 1

In ten minutes the westbound train would reach the town Euphemia Roper once vowed to never set foot in again.

Hillsdale, Michigan, was the town Euphemia—Mia to her friends—had called home longer than anywhere else in her twenty-four years, and she had left with a broken heart. Only opportunity knocking too loudly to be ignored could draw her back. For a week she would research the story that would establish her as a professional lady of letters, while she avoided encounters with the man who'd left her heart in pieces.

She twisted on her train seat and rubbed a patch of glass free of frost with her gloved fingers. The action accomplished little beyond making her hand damp through the knitted wool. The lights of Osseo had already dimmed beyond a veil of falling snow. The train gathered speed.

So did Euphemia's heart.

Muscles twitching in her legs, Euphemia tucked her

handbag under one arm and her writing portfolio under the other. Rustling pages, snapping locks and a child asking if they were there yet rose like a wave before a high wind. Euphemia stood, planning to head up the aisle to be near the door before the train stopped so she could be one of the first passengers to disembark. Others preceded her, including a child barely old enough to walk. He paused to grasp the side of her seat.

"Are you lost?" Euphemia leaned toward the boy.

Someone should be frantically in search of the little one.

"Nana?" His quivering lower lip protruded.

"Uh-oh. Don't cry. I'll find your mo—"

The train whistle blasted its mournful call into the night. Women exclaimed. Euphemia jumped, and the child let out a howl loud enough to wake any passenger still asleep after the whistle blast.

"You poor baby." Euphemia set her handbag and portfolio on her empty seat and slipped into a crouch before the boy, her skirt billowing around her. "I'll find your momma." She raised her voice. "Is anyone here missing a—"

With the cacophony of a hundred metal sheets slamming together, the train shuddered to a halt. The car floor bucked. Baby, Euphemia and luggage tumbled across the aisle. Passengers screamed.

"We've wrecked," someone shouted.

The car rocked on its wheels. More cases fell. More passengers shrieked.

"We're going to derail."

"We're going to die."

"Fire!"

No more than the usual tendrils of coal smoke filled the car, but passengers stampeded for the door. One wrist throbbing, Euphemia snatched up the child and dove back into her seat. The contents of her handbag crunched under her feet. Her writing case had remained on the seat.

"Help me." A woman's cries rose above the hubbub of wailing, shouting, shoving passengers. "My leg. I can't walk. I can't move."

"Stay here." Euphemia laid the child on the seat. She picked up her writing case before she headed for the back of the car and the crying woman.

"Where are you?" Euphemia called.

Banging, wailing and bellowing drowned out the woman's reply.

Euphemia's heart leaped into her throat, pulsing hard enough to choke her. She paused to take a deep, steadying breath. Calm would accomplish more than panic. Enough chaos reigned behind her. She didn't need to add to it.

She took a step toward where she thought she heard the woman crying for help. The car tilted. A piece of luggage slammed into her legs. She grabbed for a seatback to steady herself, and pain blazed through her left wrist. Left—something to thank the Lord for. She tucked her writing case beneath her left forearm in order to free her right hand. It was all right, strong, capable of groping in the near total darkness between the seats for the woman who had been sobbing and calling for help or for anyone else unable to ask for assistance. Three seats lay between Euphemia and the end of the railroad car. She checked on, between and under each one.

"Ma'am?" Euphemia shouted above the ruckus of what seemed like more people than the car, or the entire train, could have carried. "Are you there?"

Behind her, a baby wailed. The one she'd found or someone else's. Must get back to him, find his momma or nurse. But first the woman.

She reached the last row. Her questing fingers touched a shoulder between the seats and wedged against the rear exit.

A hand clasped hers. "You've got to help me."

"I'll do what I can." Euphemia stooped to get her arm under the woman. "Can you lean on me?"

"I think my leg is broke." The fingers gripped Euphemia's nearly hard enough to break her bones. "I can't walk. I gotta get out of here."

"We all do." Euphemia freed her hand.

"Don't leave me."

"I must go so I can get help." Euphemia took a step back, turned and headed up the aisle, calling, "Any strong men here? There's a woman here who needs to be carried."

No response from inside the car. Outside, a few lights bobbed, perhaps a promise of rescue on its way.

She paused at her seat. The toddler still lay there. He no longer sobbed or so much as whimpered. Surely such quiet wasn't normal for a child.

"Anyone missing a baby?" She grimaced at how ridiculous the words sounded when shouted.

If someone mislaid her child, she would be doing the asking. Yet no cries of a frantic mother—or anyone else seeking a little boy—rose above the ruckus. That made two people to help—the woman and the baby.

Euphemia patted the toddler. "I'll be right back."

She started up the aisle. "I need someone to carry a woman. Please."

Someone grabbed her arm. "Can you help me, young lady?" The voice and the hand shook.

"Of course. Hold on to my arm." Euphemia continued toward the exit.

"Can someone help me with these children?" A woman yelled, voice breaking.

"I can't find my cane." The voice cracked from the throat of a man who sounded ancient.

"I'll return to help you shortly," Euphemia assured the supplicants.

She must get her current charge off of the train, help those she could and find help for those she couldn't. She must work fast. Too much smoke filled the air now, and that stench of hot metal twisted her insides like one of those new pretzel rolls. Judging from the smell, the train was on fire.

"I said it would burn." The voice rose to a shriek. "Out. We gotta get out of here."

Passengers began to push and shove. The hubbub grew deafening, no voice loud enough to rise above another.

"Quiet, all of you." Deep and authoritative, a man's voice penetrated the chaos. "We will get you off one at a time, and it will be faster if you stay calm."

Euphemia's knees buckled. Breath snagged in her throat. Spots danced before her eyes.

She knew that voice. Not so long ago, her ears strained to hear it calling her name, murmuring he loved her. Now, the last thing she wanted was to push forward with the rest of the passengers and meet him face-to-face.

She freed her arm from the older lady's hold and tapped the shoulder of a man in front of her. "Will you please help this lady? I need to assist others."

Euphemia placed the elderly lady's fingers in his and then slipped past her to the woman with the children.

"Stay here for a few more minutes," she said. "It's too crowded up there right now."

"But the train's on fire." The woman sobbed as loudly as her offspring. "We'll burn alive."

"No, no. The fire is a long way off." Euphemia smiled to make her assurance more convincing.

* * *

A dozen cars lay between the engine boiler and theirs. With the wetness of the snow, the fire shouldn't spread quickly. Wind might carry sparks, though, and then—

She tugged a woolly cap more snuggly around the younger child's ears. "I'll be back in a minute to help get your children up to the door. A m-man is there helping people down."

She swung away. Pulling on this boy's cap reminded her of the toddler. She must look to his safety. And the woman with the broken leg still needed aid.

The old man caught hold of her coat sleeve. "My cane. I can't find my cane. You said you'd help me find my cane."

"I did, yes." She found it amid a pile of small parcels wedged beneath a seat across the aisle, yanked it free and handed it to the gentleman. "Will you be all right from here? I have a baby to look after and a woman with a broken leg."

She didn't wait for the man to answer. The toddler had begun to wail.

She reached him and patted his back. "I'm here, baby. We'll find your mother. She's got to be here somewhere."

Once again she felt around on the dirty and rather wet floor, gathering up what objects she encountered and shoving them into her handbag. If they proved not to be hers, she would seek to locate the owners later.

"All right, then." She shoved a bottle of scent, miraculously unbroken, into the bag. "Off to find your momma."

"Nana." The baby snuffled.

"Nana." Euphemia tried to lift the boy. She couldn't do it with one arm. And she wouldn't leave her writing case.

She set it down and picked up the toddler with both arms. Her left wrist protested. Hissing a gasp of pain through her teeth, she gathered up her case and headed for the front of the car, calling over her shoulder, "I'm going for help now, ma'am."

No one answered. That wasn't a good sign.

Euphemia quickened her steps. In front of her, the crowd surged forward.

"One at a time." Ayden's voice boomed above the other voices, more like a preacher's than a professor's, as full and rich as summer cream.

Euphemia closed her eyes. If only her ears could close, she could pretend he wasn't there not a score of feet away, their encounter inevitable.

"Just jump, ma'am. I'll catch you, and if I don't, the snow's as soft as a featherbed." He laughed as though this were some new game.

His light tone worked. The passengers calmed. They stopped shoving one another and lined up for their turn like obedient schoolchildren. Consequently, the line moved more quickly. Four seats, three seats, then only two seats lay between Euphemia and the doorway. With each step, her stomach knotted more tightly. Her heart beat as though threatening to pound its way out of her ribs. She should have prayed she could avoid Ayden. She should have dyed her hair and pretended to be someone else. She should have—

"Next?" Ayden directed.

Euphemia opened her eyes. She was next, or rather the child was next.

She hastened to the doorway. "Take this child. I'll return." She spoke in breathless accents.

"You need to stay with your child, ma'am," Ayden said. He didn't recognize her—yet.

She leaned down. "Take him. He's heavy."

"Ma'am, you can't—"

Squirming now, the toddler slipped from Euphemia's

one-armed hold. Ayden caught him and shot an annoyed glance Euphemia's way. Light from a lantern hanging from the side of the car shone on his face, etched every strong, chiseled bone like a sculptor's tool. A knitted hat covered most of his thick, dark hair. His deep blue eyes widened. His mouth gaped.

"Mia?" He barely whispered his pet name for her.

*Mia, mi amore,* he had dubbed her throughout their courtship.

A lump rose in her throat. The lantern light blurred, and she spun on her heel. "Others. I need help with others. There's a woman in here with a broken leg."

"Whose baby is this?" he shouted after her.

"I don't know-ow." She choked on the tightness in her throat.

"Mia."

The baby's wails drowned anything else he might have said to her. The crying grew fainter. Ayden must be moving away from the train. Good. She could help the woman with the children. But she couldn't help the woman with the injured leg on her own.

She reached the mother and took the hand of one of the children. "I can help you outside now."

She led the child to the doorway. "Stay there. I'll lift you down."

She glanced down. Without steps or platform, the ground looked a long way away. Without assistance, she was going to fall flat on her face.

"Mia, wait." Ayden sprinted across the snow-laden ground as though it were flat, dry pavement. "I'll catch you."

She'd rather fall flat on her face or stay in the train than have him anywhere near her, but to her right, the front of the train blazed like a bonfire. Heat reached back on every gust of wind.

She jumped.

Ayden caught her around the waist and held her suspended above the snow. "You're too thin."

"And you're rude. Now set me down." She pushed at his chest with her portfolio.

He set her down. "Straight ahead. Pa's just arrived with the sleigh. We'll take these people home."

"I thought you might."

"You can come, too, you know."

She shook her head. "Not a good idea. I'm staying at the boardinghouse."

"I expect it's already full." He moved past her to lift down the children and their mother.

Euphemia didn't move. "I have a reservation."

"Did you intend to stop here, ma'am?" Ayden asked the mother.

"We were going to my parents in Chicago." She sobbed as hard as her two children. "I don't know nobody here."

"That's all right. You can stay with us. Mia, will you take one of the children and show this lady to our sleigh? It's about a hundred feet straight ahead with the two lamps on it." He started toward another car.

"Wait," Euphemia called. "There's another woman in there. She's injured. She says she can't walk." And she'd lost sight of the toddler she'd promised to reunite with his family.

"I'll get her." Ayden hoisted himself inside the car.

Euphemia gave the mother and her children a reassuring smile. "I'll help you all get through this snow to the Goswells' sleigh. You'll be safe there."

"I don't know, ma'am." The woman clutched her children to her skirts. "They're strangers."

"You can trust them." She grimaced. "Not that you have any reason to trust me."

Somehow, that remark seemed to reassure the woman. She released her hold on the taller of the two children, a girl inadequately clothed for the weather. "Can you help her? I've never seen such snow."

"I have. It's like walking through a bag of flour," Euphemia said.

"Cold flour," the girl added through her snuffles.

Euphemia took her hand. "Really cold flour. I hope you can walk. You're too grown up for me to carry you."

"I'm seven."

"Really grown up." Euphemia clutched the child's mittened fingers and started toward the twin carriage lamps suspended from a sleigh, no doubt the one she had taken numerous of rides in over the years, tucked up between Ayden and his younger sister, or his mother, or just him…

She slammed the door on those memories and trudged forward. She must get these children and their mother to the Goswells' sleigh. She must find that toddler's people. Once she accomplished those tasks, she could find transportation into Hillsdale.

Plan made, she continued to tramp through the snow. Her feet felt like the packed-down stuff, heavy, solid, immovable. She didn't want to see Mr. Goswell any more than she wanted to see Ayden again. He had been a father to her, more so than her own, who disappeared intermittently in pursuit of nameless dreams until he disappeared permanently. Her father's last words to her had been, *I'll be back.* Mr. Goswell's had been, *I'm so disappointed in the two of you it hurts.*

Her response was nothing she was proud to recall, and a fresh wave of guilt stabbed her as he loomed before her, his hair gray rather than mahogany-brown, his eyes as blue, his smile as warm. "Euphemia Roper, what a sight for sore eyes. I knew you'd be back."

"I'm not really." She kept her tone neutral. "Ayden sent me over with these people."

Mr. Goswell squeezed her shoulder. "Good. You'll stay with us."

"No, I—"

"I have that little one tucked up until we find his family. And who do we have here?"

"Some passengers who don't have a place to stay in Hillsdale."

"Yes, they do—with us." Mr. Goswell crouched to be eye to eye with the children. "Would you like to come to our house for soup and biscuits?"

The children stood in silence, turning into little snowmen beneath the tumbling flakes.

"I—I don't have much money," the mother protested.

"They won't want money." Euphemia touched the woman's arm. "I know these people. They have lots of room and will feed you until you cry for mercy."

*Kind, generous, godly,* all words to describe the Goswell family. She hadn't wanted to leave them behind, not permanently. She and Ayden were supposed to return to Hillsdale for the holidays, but Ayden chose to stay permanently.

Instead of choosing to love her.

She shook off the hurt like snow accumulating on her coat and held out her hand to draw the woman forward. "Is Mrs. Goswell in the kitchen already?"

"The minute we heard the wreck." Mr. Goswell returned his attention to the children. "Would you like a sleigh ride?"

The children nodded. Their mother made protesting noises in her throat.

Mr. Goswell glanced up at Euphemia. "Will, uh, you stay to help me with these little ones?"

"I need to look for the baby's mother, or whoever should have had charge of him." Euphemia stepped back. Her foot sank into a pile of soft snow, and the crystallized wetness tumbled over the top of her boot. "Perhaps this lady can help."

Mr. Goswell rested his hand on Euphemia's shoulder. "She already has her own two, and you shouldn't be charging off on your own through this crowd at night. It's not safe."

"I've been in worse," Euphemia said.

"I'm happy to see to the little one to pay my way," the woman said.

"There's no need," Mr. Goswell began.

"That's an excellent idea." Euphemia recognized the woman's need to contribute to spare her pride. "If you go to your house, I'll know where to find you when I find the baby's family." Without further ado, she yanked her foot from the snowdrift and headed toward the train, the worst of the crowd and the blazing fire creeping back from the engine.

"I'll be back," Mr. Goswell shouted after her, but she continued without looking back.

The going grew rougher with each step. Snow clung to her skirt and petticoats, weighing them down. More snow filled her boots. She should have gone into town with Mr. Goswell. His wife would have all the fires going and hot coffee on the stove. But duty called.

Euphemia approached a group of women huddled together. "Are any of you missing a child about a year and a half old?"

The women stared at her, their faces blank with shock in the flickering light of the burning train.

"No," one finally answered.

"If you hear of anyone, send them to the Goswell house." Euphemia turned away.

She set about asking another group and another. The answer remained the same—no one had heard of anyone seeking a baby like the one she described. Plenty of people sought loved ones. They wandered through the snow and stench of burning coal like sheep without their shepherd despite the flocks of townspeople who moved through them, talking, soothing, gathering the stranded passengers to transport them into town. Every conversation focused on the trains. Off their schedules, the east- and westbound locomotives had crashed.

"The eastbound didn't have no headlight," one man said again and again. "It didn't have no headlight."

Frozen to her bones, Euphemia paused on snow packed as hard as ice from scores of feet. Mere yards away, the trains blazed with some of their cars broken free of their couplings and toppled over, others leaning at a precarious angle, and the farther back ones, like the one she'd ridden in, appearing undamaged.

"What a mess." She took in each detail, committing them to memory.

If only she knew how to take photographs and owned a camera, this incident would do more for her journalism career on the *Ladies' Monthly Fashion* than any other story she had written. She should take notes, write down snatches of conversation. The conflagration provided enough light.

Careful of her throbbing wrist, she opened her writing case and extracted a pencil and paper. *Stray toddler. Woman broken leg. Old woman...*

"What are you doing?" Ayden snatched the pencil from her gloved fingers.

"I'm taking notes so I don't forget any of my impressions." She held out her hand. "Please give me back my pencil."

He did so. "You always were taking notes on something." He smiled. A dimple flashed in his left cheek, and her heart performed a somersault inside her ribs.

No, no, no, she would not succumb to the charm of that smile, that boyish dent in his cheek, his deep, resonant voice.

She took a step away from him. "I should get into town, I suppose. I heard something about the churches opening up to help stranded passengers. Perhaps I can find that boy's people there. Did you get that woman help? I suppose Dr. Clark is run off his feet help—"

"Hush." Ayden laid a gloved finger across her lips. "You don't need to be nervous around me, Mia."

She laughed. "Why would you think I'm nervous around you?"

"Because you're talking too much." His smile faded. "And to answer your question—no, I did not help that woman. She wasn't there."

# *Chapter 2*

Mia's eyes widened, dark against her face washed of color in the lantern light and snow reflection. Ayden gazed into those green eyes, and his heart performed an acrobatic flip inside his chest. It was perhaps the tenth or so flip his heart had performed since he looked up at the doorway of the railroad carriage and saw her, the woman he had loved for nearly six years.

*She's come home,* his heart had cried.

Even if she was, he did not—would not—love Mia now, whatever his heart believed. Charmaine Finney—daughter of the director of the Hillsdale College classics department, who just happened to be Ayden's superior—was the lady in his life. She, not Euphemia Roper, held the key to his future happiness.

Yet he could not forget how Mia turned him inside out from the day he met her and kept him off balance until the day she dealt him the blow that toppled his world. He'd rebuilt that world over the past year and a half. One look into her heart-shaped face, framed in some kind of white fur on her hood, should not send him reeling like a man struck on the head. He intended to marry Charmaine, not let Mia tie him into knots again.

He turned his face to the cold blast of wind. "Let's get into town. Perhaps we can find that baby's people there."

The sooner he got her into town, the sooner he could forget about his misbehaving heart.

"There's no room on the sleigh."

"I have a horse."

She flashed a glare from beneath her lashes. "You expect me to ride with you?"

"It won't be the first time."

The words spilled out, evoking happier times of summer picnics and winter sledding parties.

She turned away. "I'll walk."

"Don't be a fool, Mia." He slipped his hand beneath her elbow and guided her toward the edge of the thinning crowd along the length of the wrecked westbound train. "You can ride behind me."

She would still have to hold onto him somehow but not as closely as she would if she rode in front of him.

"It's less than ten minutes," he reminded her.

She said nothing, simply slogged through the snow with her head bent against the wind. She held her left arm at a crook, hugging that writing case of hers like it was an infant, except her hand didn't touch it. Her fingers inside their glove stood straight out, as though they had frozen stiff in that position.

"Mia?" he asked as they tramped through the snow to his mount. "Is your hand all right?"

"My hand is perfectly all right, thank you." Her tone sounded as stiff as her fingers looked.

"Then let me have it so I can help you mount."

She pressed the writing case more tightly against her front. "I can mount once you're up."

"That would be interesting to watch if I were attending a farce. But since this is reality, I'm lifting you up."

She took a step back.

Ayden sighed. "How old are you now? Twenty-four?"

"January first, yes. Why?"

"I thought perhaps you'd outgrow that stubbornness by now."

The corners of her mouth twitched upward. "It might be worse."

"It's nothing to be proud of."

He sounded like a curmudgeon. A year and a half of persuading students to pay attention to his lectures must have aged him beyond his twenty-eight years.

"Mia, what are you afraid of?" he asked in a gentler voice.

"I'm not afraid of anything, Ayden Goswell. I would simply rather not spend more time with you than necessary."

"This falls under the necessary category."

No longer giving her a chance to protest, he picked her up by her waist, a waist that felt too slender through her thick coat and all the other things ladies wore, and hoisted her onto the back of his chestnut gelding. She never released her hold on that writing case or her handbag. The latter smacked him in the face. The horse, which was old, a little overweight and steady, remained motionless through the ordeal of Mia arranging her skirts and then Ayden mounting.

"Hold on," he directed.

A tug on his coat told him she held the fabric and no more. He set the mount to an even, slow pace to accommodate the extra person perched behind him. All the way past the burning train, mail cars flaming with their paper contents and stragglers finding their way toward Hillsdale, Ayden tried not to think about the lady perched behind him, shoved memories away with images of Charmaine with her sunshine-yellow hair and big blue eyes. She was as sweet-tempered as Mia was stubborn.

With each jolt of the horse's hooves through the snow-laden ground, a corner of Mia's writing case jabbed Ayden's shoulder blade. The rest of the time, the hard leather portfolio rode between them, interrupting his attempts to focus on Charmaine with its constant reminder of why he and Mia had broken their engagement.

"Shall I leave you at First Church?" he asked, his voice harsh in the quiet space between wrecked trains and town.

"Th-that would be b-best." She spoke through teeth clattering together loudly enough for Ayden to hear.

"Are you cold?"

Stupid question. Of course she was cold.

"Perhaps I should take you to the boardinghouse first," he suggested. "They'll have a fire and you can change into something dry.

"I have nothing to change into. My luggage is back on the train."

The fire would soon destroy her personal effects if it wasn't stopped.

"I'm not your co-concern, Ayden. I haven't been since you de-decided to stay here instead of going to Boston with me." Even through her cold-induced stammer, the acid dripped from her voice hot enough to melt the snow around them.

Ayden flinched. He jerked the reins, and the gelding halted.

In an instant, Mia slid to the ground. "There's a wagon ahead. I'll see if they'll give me a lift."

"Mia, don't." Ayden leaned down to rest his hand on her arm.

She drew her breath in through her teeth and jerked away from him.

Ayden leaped from the horse and grasped her shoulders. "What's wrong?"

"Nothing, I'm sure. Just a bit of a sprain."

Ayden took her left hand in his. "You said your hand was all right."

"It's my wrist. I fell when the trains collided."

He ground his teeth. "Splitting hairs, Mia, *mi amo*—"

No, she wasn't his love any longer, though the idea that she had stayed to help so many people despite an injured arm reminded him of one of the many reasons why she had been his love. She was strong and courageous, caring and generous.

"I didn't want you to fuss," Mia said. "And you can't do anything about it here in the snow."

"I'll get you to Dr. Clark before I do anything else."

"I must find that baby's family."

"At least let me hold your portfolio."

She ignored his request and started along the ruts the wagon had left in its wake. Snow was beginning to fill them, but it was light and fluffy, easy to walk over. It silenced their footfalls and the gelding's hooves. Ahead of them, light from houses and businesses reflected off the whiteness to make the world glow. The wind carried the scent of wood smoke with its promise of warm fires, hot soup and hotter coffee.

Ayden lengthened his stride and then slowed again so he remained at Mia's side. "Will you be all right if I leave you at Dr. Clark's?"

"Yes, of course." She walked with her head bent and both arms around her writing case.

"I'll help you find that child's people," Ayden offered.

"I'd rather you didn't."

Although she didn't say so, the certainty of the meaning behind her refusal of his help rang loudly and clearly through the night. And they stung like the pellet of white crystals against his face.

"It's been eighteen months, Mia," he burst out. "Surely after that much time you can forgive me."

"Yes, I can—forgive and forget. Or did you think I came back here to see you?"

"I wouldn't be so foolish. But you must have known you were likely to see me here."

"I expected to be able to get away from you if I did." She picked up her snow-crusted skirts in her good hand and increased her speed.

Ayden let her walk ahead of him. She had always carried too much pride on her shoulders. Far be it from him to remove it. He had dealt it too much damage the summer she finished her education.

With Mia walking a yard in front of Ayden, they finished the last half mile distance into town. The closer they drew to Hillsdale, the brighter shone the lights. Nearly every house and business glowed with candles, oil lamps or lanterns in windows and hanging outside. First Church stood out the brightest and loudest. Wagons and sleighs lined the street in front of the building. Bedraggled, snow-covered people swarmed in and out of the front door, many crying, raging against the railroad's incompetence, and others pleading for help.

Dr. Clark's house and office lay farther on, but as they began to pass the church, the doctor himself appeared in the doorway, engaged in conversation with one of his students, Miss Liberty Judd. She was dressed in some fancy green gown and jewels sparkled in her hair, of all the ridiculous things.

Ayden closed the distance between Mia and himself. "You may as well stop here." He reached out his hand but didn't touch so much as her coat sleeve. "If you need anything while you're here, don't hesitate to come ask us. You know we'll do anything for you."

Except for the one thing she had asked of him.

He winced inside as he displayed a smile.

"Thank you." She flashed him her quick, brilliant grin and swung toward the church.

Dr. Clark and Liberty would take care of Mia, attend to her injured wrist, get her to her room for the night and anything else she needed. He headed home to help his parents and sister with the woman and three children they had gathered from the wreck.

He led his horse to the stable behind their back garden and rubbed him down. Stroking the gelding's chestnut mane reminded Ayden how he had purchased that particular horse because the color matched Mia's shining hair. In spite of that illogical reason for buying a mount, the gelding had proved to be a fine animal, placid and biddable, not at all like Mia.

Smiling at the comparison, Ayden scooped a measure of grain into the horse's feed trough and crossed the yard to the house. Light blazed through a window in the back door. He yanked it open and sighed with contentment at the heat and aromas of chicken soup, brewing coffee and baking bread that surrounded him.

His sister, Rosalie, greeted him from the stove. "Go change before you catch a chill."

"Thank you, Mother." He tugged one of Rosalie's dark curls tumbling down her back. "Where is she anyway?"

"Upstairs getting those poor children and their mother some dry clothes so we can feed them."

"So Pa got home all right."

"Yes and headed out to see who else he could gather up." Rosalie set aside the spoon she was using to stir a pot of soup and faced him, her blue eyes dancing. "Where's Mia?"

Ayden suppressed a groan. "I should have known Pa would tell you all she's in town."

"He was bursting with the news."

"Such a vulgar expression. If you'd go to the college, you'd learn better—"

Rosalie whacked the back of his hand with her heavy wooden spoon. "Not tonight, Ayden." She tossed the spoon into the dry sink of dirty dishes and selected another one from a hook on the wall. "Go get yourself into dry clothes and come back for something hot to eat while you tell us all about Mia."

"Not tonight. Or any night. I'm too weary from pulling people out of railroad cars and need to get up to the church to see what else I can do to help."

"I'll go with you if Pa gets back soon. Fletcher has been at First Church since they started taking stranded passengers there." A smile played about her lips, and her eyes softened as she referred to the man who'd been courting her for two years. "He asked me to come with him, but I didn't want to leave Mom home alone."

"Wise of you," Ayden said.

*For once.* He wouldn't say that aloud, even though the words spoke the truth.

His sister was kind, intelligent and beautiful. She also followed her heart more than was of good judgment. Her adoration of Fletcher Lambert was on the list of poor judgments. Wisdom and common sense were not among Rosalie's many good qualities.

But she was right. Tonight was not the time to poke at her about her future.

"I'm happy to hear Fletch is at the church," Ayden said. "It looked rather chaotic there."

"I expect it was worse at the wreck." Rosalie's eyes clouded. "Was it terrible?"

"It could have been worse. I think we managed to save most everyone. If we didn't, they were beyond our help, I'm sad to say."

Rosalie gave him a sidelong glance as she lifted a spoonful of soup to her lips. "Mia wasn't injured, was she?"

"Her wrist is hurting her."

Yet she had continued to help others and seek that baby's family in spite of her pain.

Rosalie frowned at him. "If she's injured, you should have brought her here."

"She didn't want to come." Ayden turned away, started toward the inside kitchen door and paused there, his hand on the latch. "She wants no more to do with me than I want to do with her, so that's an end to it."

If only his heart would resume its normal operations instead of interfering with his breathing each time someone spoke Mia's name.

# Chapter 3

Euphemia scowled at the bandage the doctor had wound around her left wrist, immobilizing it. "I'm not much use to anyone with only one free hand."

"You should be in a warm, dry bed with someone helping you, not the other way around," Dr. Clark told her. "If you don't get out of those wet clothes soon, a sprained wrist won't be your only trouble."

"Of course, Doctor, but there's just one problem with that." Euphemia smiled sweetly. "I don't have any dry clothes."

"Then find a hot fire to stand in front of and steam yourself like a dumpling." He grinned despite the lines of fatigue etching his face, then he turned away to attend to a child with a woolen scarf wrapped around her foot instead of a shoe. "What happened here?"

"I loozed my shoe." The child's rosebud mouth quivered. The sight reminded Euphemia of the toddler on the train, and she touched the doctor's shoulder. "I'm sorry to interrupt you, but have you tended a woman with a broken leg?"

He didn't look up as he began to unwind the scarf. "Nothing that serious yet. Looking for someone?"

"Yes, there was—"

Blood appeared on the pink yarn of the makeshift bandage, and the child started to wail, drowning Euphemia's words.

She glanced at the pale young woman with the child, guessed from the poor quality of her dress in comparison with the girl's thick wool and fur she was a nanny or governess rather than her mother and decided not to ask her about the abandoned little boy. The young woman's pallor suggested she would be the doctor's next patient.

"Send a message to the boardinghouse if you encounter a woman with a broken leg," Euphemia said above the girl's cries of distress.

She turned and headed for the door of the church. Around her, passengers accepted blankets, dry clothes and cups of hot coffee and tea from townsfolk.

The pastor of First Church offered the building for anyone who had no place to stay. "Though we're getting crowded."

"So's the hotel," someone called. "Try Mrs. Greene's boardinghouse."

"I only have one room left, and it's reserved." Mrs. Greene, who had owned the boardinghouse practically from the founding of the town two decades earlier, stood in the doorway to the sanctuary. "If she don't show up in another ten minutes, I'm giving the room to someone else."

"I'm here." Euphemia wound her way around knots of people gathered in the entryway and reached out her right hand to the boardinghouse keeper. "I'm here, Mrs. Greene. Please don't give my room away."

"You can stay with us, Mia," Mr. Goswell said from behind her.

Euphemia smiled at him over her shoulder. "Thank you, but I'd rather you gave the space to people who truly need it."

"We already have," Mr. Goswell said. "That woman and her children will be staying in Frank's room."

He referred to their elder son, who now lived in Chicago.

"But we could put you up with Rosalie," he continued. "I wouldn't be able to put a stranger there."

"Of course you can't. But—" Euphemia cradled her injured wrist and writing case with her right arm. If Ayden weren't there, she would go in an instant. Losing Ayden's family had been nearly as difficult as losing him.

Which was precisely why she could not stay in their house and accept their kindness and generosity of spirit, the hope she read in Mr. Goswell's face. She couldn't hurt them again any more than she wanted to be hurt again herself.

"I think we're all better off if I stay at the boardinghouse." She turned away and skirted a knot of people to reach the boardinghouse proprietress. "I'm here."

Mrs. Greene's eyes gleamed in her moon face. "I saw you. Gonna put you up in your old attic room. I know it's tiny, but had to put families in the bigger rooms."

"That's quite all right." Euphemia tightened the corners of her mouth. "I'll pay the old rate." Before the woman could argue with her, Euphemia spun toward the door.

Mr. Goswell remained near the opening, and Ayden had joined him, holding a boy of about five or six. His eyes met Euphemia's across the room.

For a moment, the weight of one of those railroad cars seemed to crush upon her chest and Euphemia couldn't breathe at the sight of Ayden holding a child so protectively in his arms. If only things had gone differently, if only he had taken the teaching position in Boston instead of remaining in Hillsdale, he could be holding their little boy like that. But he'd broken his promise, made a choice that took them in different directions.

The scene blurred before Euphemia's eyes, and she turned away.

She entered the sanctuary. People bunched together on the pews, many slumped or stretched out in repose, if not sleep. Volunteers from the town moved about, distributing blankets and cups of steaming liquids. Euphemia passed the little girl with the injured foot and her pallid governess. The former lay on a pew, wrapped in a crocheted blanket, her bandaged toes sticking out. The latter sat beside her charge, her hands in darned, black gloves folded in her lap, her pale eyes fixed on the altar.

Euphemia slipped through the door beside the choir loft and toward the rear of the church. The odor of burned candle wax and old song books stung her nostrils, scents as familiar to her as the college library but not as comforting. These aromas pricked her conscience.

She hadn't been to church in far too many weeks, distracted by her pursuit of following her dream. Just like her father. Except she never made promises she didn't intend to keep. And she would return to this church on Sunday and thank the Lord for preserving her life and that of so many others.

She opened the rear door to a blast of snow-thickened wind.

"Miss? Miss, a moment, please?" The high, thin voice

battled the whine of the wind around the corner of the building.

Euphemia slammed the door and turned back. "Yes?"

"M-may I speak with you a moment?" Light from the sanctuary shone on the pale hair and face of the governess.

Legs suddenly as stiff as a snow sculpture's, Euphemia retraced her steps down the passageway and joined the young woman just inside the church. "How may I help you?"

"I—well, I was wondering... I couldn't help but overhear..." The young woman twisted her hands together and gazed past Euphemia's left ear. "Some people offered you a place to stay, and I'm afraid my employers won't like me keeping their daughter amongst the hoi polloi—that's what they'll call this—" She swept one hand out to indicate the assembled persons sleeping on the pews. "But the hotel and boardinghouse are full. So I was wondering... We can compensate you, of course. My employers are generous when it comes to their daughter's needs."

"You'll compensate me for what?" Euphemia asked.

The young woman stared at Euphemia as though she were a rather dull-witted child. "Why, for you to give up your room in the boardinghouse and stay with your friends."

Euphemia's wrist throbbed. Her head ached. She could no longer feel her toes inside their sodden stockings and boots. She wanted nothing more than to steam herself dry beside a fire and then go to sleep in a real bed. But not a bed at the Goswell house.

The governess had recommenced twisting her hands together hard enough for her fingertip to protrude through one of the darns in her gloves. She must be poorly compensated, or need her wages for other more important matters, to wear such shabby gloves in the winter. Were her employers ungenerous enough to dismiss her for not taking good enough care of their daughter—despite the circumstances?

The mere possibility kept Euphemia's mouth shut until she found the courage to answer. "All right. Tell Mrs. Greene you may have my room."

"Thank you." The young woman smiled, and her eyes glowed like sunlit silver. "I'll pray extra for you for this kindness." Back straight and steps light, she hastened back to wake her young charge.

Euphemia retreated to the entryway. The Goswells had gone. She must, like a supplicant, arrive at their door in the middle of the night.

"How humiliating," she muttered.

The alternative—remaining there to sleep on a pew in her wet garments—was less acceptable. For warmth and food and a dry bed, she could swallow her pride just this once and risk encounters with Ayden—or perhaps not.

She headed down the street. Despite a new moon and the predawn hour, lanterns hung outside houses and the glow of the snow lit her way along a route she knew well, a mere three blocks to the church.

In the night, the house looked the same—square and solid. Wood smoke scented the air around it, and a dog barked from beyond the front door.

Euphemia skirted the house to knock on the kitchen door. Ayden was less likely to be in the kitchen than the front parlor or study.

She was wrong. He opened the door.

"Mia." He jerked back a step. "I didn't think we'd see you again."

"I apologize. It wasn't my intention." She avoided looking at his deep blue eyes, so warm in the cold night. "I gave up my place in the boardinghouse to a governess and her charge."

"You would." His voice held a tender note that brought tears to Euphemia's eyes.

She was tired was all, worn to a thread from the travel and the wreck and her aching wrist.

"You know you're welcome here." He waved to a brightly lit kitchen smelling of coffee and bread. "Come in."

Euphemia entered. Not until she pushed back her hood and shoved clumps of frozen hair out of her face did she notice the blonde seated at the table peeling potatoes. She stood, revealing a trim figure in a merino dress over what had to be a crinoline to appear so crisp at that hour and a chignon without a hair out of place.

"This is Charmaine Finney," Ayden said, "a friend."

"You're a very good friend to be here helping in the middle of the night," Euphemia responded. "Pleased to meet you, Miss Finney." She pulled off her glove and held out her hand.

Miss Finney touched her fingertips. "When I heard how many people the Goswells had taken in, I just had to come and help. Father wouldn't have anyone in our house, I'm sad to say. He fears Mother's silver will disappear."

"Charmaine's father is director of the classics department," Ayden said as he closed the door after nodding to Charmaine.

What he didn't need to say was that the lovely lady's father was his director at the college.

"I remember Dr. Finney." Euphemia smiled at Ayden with the first genuine warmth she'd managed all night. She could afford to be friendly with him. "You should have told me you were taken. I wouldn't have worried about your parents trying to match us."

"No, you shouldn't have to." His tone was brusque. "Let me find Momma and Rosalie. I think they're in the attic digging up clothes for the children." He bolted from the kitchen like a schoolboy about to be caught in a naughty deed.

Euphemia raised her eyebrows. "I think I'll get myself some coffee and steam dry by the stove here, if you won't be inconvenienced by it." She removed her cloak and hung it on a hook by the door beside half a dozen wraps.

"Why should I mind? I'm a guest here, too." Miss Finney resumed peeling potatoes. "Do you know where to find cups, or should I help you?"

"I know, if nothing's changed." Without releasing her left-armed hold on her writing case, Euphemia selected a thick mug from a cupboard and lifted the pot from the back of the stove.

The brew streamed into the cup as thick and dark as oil. No doubt the Goswells kept milk in the cellar this time of year and she could fetch some to dilute the coffee, but she didn't bother. She needed the stimulating brew to keep her wits about her now that she was face-to-face with the new lady in Ayden's life.

She still woke aching with the loss of him, and he happily courted another female.

Charmaine was beautiful with her pale blond perfection, eyes the color of a summer lake and skin as pure and smooth as that of a porcelain doll. Besides her looks, she must be kind, too, to give up a night's sleep to help the Goswells prepare food for their household of unexpected guests.

The coffee turned to acid on her lips, burned in her stomach, and she set the cup on the table, too weary to hold the crockery any longer. She slumped in one of the kitchen chairs and held out her bandaged wrist. "I don't think I can help you peel potatoes, but maybe I can cut them."

"I think you should be in a bed, Miss Roper." Charmaine smiled. "Don't look so surprised. Of course I know who you are. My father talked about you when you were in his class as a freshman at Michigan Central College before it was Hillsdale College. He said you wrote the best papers of anyone, including Ayden's."

"He was kind to me." Euphemia rested her head on her good hand. "But I don't remember you."

"I didn't go to the college. I prefer being Father's hostess and housekeeper and doing my charity work for the church."

"And being a good choice for Ayden's wife."

Charmaine wouldn't be running to a city to take on that unfeminine occupation—a career in journalism—or any other career beyond wife and mother.

Charmaine laughed. "Not quite that…yet."

The sound of voices outside the kitchen prevented Euphemia from saying more. She rose in time to meet Mrs. Goswell's voluminous, cinnamon-scented embrace.

"Mia. Oh, my, Mia Roper, you don't know how happy we are that you're here." The older woman drew back and wiped her eyes with the corner of her pristine apron. "We've prayed and prayed for you, and I knew I was right to know God promised you'd come back."

Euphemia refrained from saying God had nothing to do with her presence in their kitchen at four o'clock in the morning. At least she didn't think He did.

"I'm happy to see you, too, ma'am."

Mia was much happier now that she realized Ayden's parents couldn't want her there for a reunion between her and Ayden, a painful prospect at best.

"I see you're drinking coffee to warm up," Mrs. Goswell said. "I'll get you some soup and bread, too."

"She needs dry clothes first." Rosalie also embraced Euphemia. "Come up to my room and I'll find you something. You're a little shorter and a little thinner than I am but not by much." She slipped her arm through the crook of Euphemia's elbow and started for the door, then paused by Charmaine. "Thank you for doing all of those potatoes. Should Ayden walk you home?"

"I can stay if you need more help." Charmaine suppressed a yawn.

"You look tired after collecting all those blankets," Mrs. Goswell said. "But I'll have my husband take you in the sleigh. Not proper for you and Ayden to be out alone this time of the morning."

"And the snow looks deeper." Charmaine glanced to the doorway where Ayden now stood.

The two shared a smile, and Euphemia closed her eyes. *This should not hurt.*

She just wished "should not" and "did not" came out the same in the end. Unfortunately, her heart had wrapped itself around her windpipe, and each breath pained her.

Rosalie squeezed her arm. "Move out of the way, brother. This lady needs to change her dress."

"How's your wrist?" Ayden asked.

"Sprained and sore." Euphemia tried to smile and failed. "I'm managing."

"You always did." He moved away from the door and strode to stand behind Charmaine's chair. "If there aren't any classes tomorrow, which I doubt there will be…"

Rosalie nearly dragged Euphemia from the kitchen, allowing the door to bang shut behind her. "If there aren't classes tomorrow, he'll bring her back here to help Momma cook, and we'll all be miserable."

Euphemia blinked. "You don't like her? She seems like a nice lady."

"She is." Rosalie paused with one foot on the bottom step. "She is sweet and pretty and giving and kind and just so good at everything she does the rest of us feel like a herd of elephants in a crystal room."

"Ah, no wonder Ayden is taken with her." Euphemia managed to say the words in a neutral voice.

Rosalie snorted and started up the steps. "You'll share my room. I have a blazing fire and warm clothes for you, and I'll bring you up a tray so you don't have to see my brother until you feel more yourself."

"Do I have to see your brother at all?"

"Oh, I do hope so." Rosalie came to the top of the polished wood steps and turned right. At the end of the hallway with the strip of red turkey carpet down the center, she pushed open the door to a room with a fire crackling on the small hearth and a dressing gown and slippers toasting over a chair before the blaze. "Now that you're here, we all hope he'll change his mind about making an offer for Miss Charmaine Finney's hand in marriage and come to his senses about you."

"Um, no, Rosalie." Euphemia stumbled into the pink-and-white bedroom and held her free hand out to the flames. "I didn't come back here to renew anything with Ayden. I'm here only for my work. If not for the wreck, I would have avoided seeing any of you at all. I'm sorry to say that. You all were such a family to me, but the relationship between Ayden and me is obviously over."

"Ha. You went all stiff down there when Ayden looked at Charmaine." Rosalie adjusted a carved wooden screen across one corner. "Go in there and change into this nightgown and robe. Then I can tell you why your arrival is such an answer to prayer."

Euphemia didn't move. "I don't want to hear any such thing. I wouldn't interfere with Ayden and Charmaine even if I still wanted him to court me, which I do not. He hurt me too much."

"I know he did. But Mia—" Rosalie grasped Euphemia's hand between both of hers and gazed at her with the Goswell-blue eyes, rich in color, intense with emotion. "If I thought Ayden loved Charmaine, I would make sure you didn't interfere with their courtship. But he doesn't."

"You don't know that. He didn't love me, either, obviously." Euphemia blinked back moisture in her eyes.

Despite the five years' difference in their ages, Euphemia had wept on Rosalie's shoulder a year and a half ago.

Rosalie sighed. "I know he was beastly to you. I didn't speak to him for weeks after you left and he didn't, even after he'd promised to join you. But, Mia, him marrying Charmaine would be worse. She is a nice person, and he's courting her for all the wrong reasons, even if he won't admit it."

# Chapter 4

Ayden rested his elbows on the kitchen table, too weary to move, too awake to go to bed. At five o'clock in the morning, he may as well stay awake and begin the day. He needed to shovel snow. The horses also needed to be fed and their stalls mucked out. With all the soup she'd heated and coffee she'd brewed during the night, Ma would need more wood chopped for the stove.

Most of Hillsdale might call Ayden Professor Goswell, but he was still Wilson and Rebecca Goswell's younger son living at home. As such, he was expected to help with the chores. He tried to finish them before he headed for campus at seven-thirty in the morning. Otherwise, he found himself wielding an ax and splitter between preparing lectures and grading tests. He had to be careful to give himself time to prepare as the professor. Students, especially the female ones, concentrated more on his disheveled appearance than his history lecture.

Ah, female students. God bless Charmaine for coming into his life and protecting him from the young women who tended to leave cookies, pies and, once, a layer cake in his office. Then Charmaine came along with her sweet nature and blond beauty, and the gifts of baked goods ceased.

Of course, that wasn't the only reason he'd begun to court Charmaine. He enjoyed her company, her serenity, her kindness. Never in his life had he been so comfortable in the presence of a female, not even Mia.

Mia was anything but a comfortable female to be around. She voiced opinions. She argued. She was single-minded about accomplishing a task—but wasn't always careful about how she got there.

But he had loved her to distraction. He had wept when she left Hillsdale with a vow never to return. So now, when he was all but engaged to Charmaine, Mia had reneged on her promise to never see him again and had leaped off that wrecked train.

"Oh, Lord Jesus, what do I do?" He didn't realize he spoke the prayer of desperation aloud until a hand dropped onto his shoulder.

"You might want to try a few hours of sleep," Ma suggested.

Ayden smiled up at her. "Too much to do. The horses, the shoveling, avoiding Mia."

"That's going to be rather difficult." Ma went to the stove and began to make coffee. "This is a fine big house, but it's not that big. Unless you stay away from dawn to bedtime, you're bound to see her."

"I've got plenty of work to keep me away." He rose. "I'll see to the horses and the shoveling."

"You don't want some coffee and breakfast first?"

"It'll taste even better after hard work in the cold."

Maybe the physical labor would clear his head of the

image of Mia's arresting face surrounded by the snow-crusted fur trimming her hood. It was surely the same hood that had surrounded her face on many a ride in the sleigh or sledding expedition—like the one when he first kissed her.

He stamped his feet into his boots and stalked out of the house, away from the heat and into the cold. He closed the door behind him, wishing he could so easily close the door on memories of how happy she had made him.

"Think about Charmaine." He spoke the words aloud, then repeated them.

While raking soiled straw from the horses' stalls, he focused on Charmaine's face, her curls the color of ripe wheat, her eyes like the sky on a clear day in August, her lips the hue of a luscious strawberry—lips he hadn't yet kissed. Maybe he should. Maybe that would once and for all drive memories of Mia from his head.

But he couldn't get her out of his head while she slept under his parents' roof.

He forked fresh straw into stalls and hay into mangers with so much vigor the carriage team backed against the walls of their stalls like they expected him to grab their manes with the tines and haul them behind the stable. His own mount snorted and stamped, as though more than a little sympathetic.

"Charmaine is charming," Ayden mused aloud as he grabbed the shovel and attacked the snow drifting across the walkways. "She will make a perfect hostess." He flung snow into piles no doubt Rosalie would diminish to produce one of her snowmen. "She's had a great deal of practice."

Charmaine had played hostess for her father since her mother's death three years earlier. And Professor Finney entertained a great deal. It was expected of him as the head of the history department at the college. And Ayden was expected to attend as the newest lecturer awaiting Finney's approval for the position to become permanent.

A shovelful of snow sailed off the walk and struck the kitchen window, then tumbled atop one of Ma's lilac bushes. Two branches snapped beneath the onslaught.

Ma yanked open the back door. "I think you've done enough shoveling, Ayden. You should get yourself in here and warm up before you do any more damage."

"Yes, ma'am." He set the shovel beside the back door, then gathered an armload of firewood before shouldering his way into the kitchen.

The aromas of fresh-brewed coffee, frying ham and potatoes and baking apples and cinnamon set his mouth to watering and his stomach growling. After dumping the firewood into the box, he removed his boots and coat and crossed the room to slide a stack of plates from the cupboard. "Should I set these in the dining room for you?"

"Thank you, and get a fire going." Ma didn't look up from flipping sliced potatoes in a skillet. "Then maybe you could go wake up that sleepyhead sister of yours."

Ayden paused in the doorway and faced his mother with a shake of his head. "I don't think that's a good idea."

"Why not?" Ma drew her silver-flecked eyebrows together.

Ayden let the kitchen door swing shut behind him. She would work it out. If the creak of floorboards overhead was any indication, Rosalie was already awake. She must be trying to let Mia sleep because no voices drifted through the ceiling plaster. Kind of her, but then, Rosalie was nothing if not kind. If only she'd go to the college or find a beau more worthy of her lively goodness.

He set the plates on the table with a clatter of crockery, then stooped before the hearth. A fire had been laid. All he needed to do was crumple newspaper and wood shavings atop the logs and set a match to the kindling. They ignited with a whoosh and blaze of heat. He held his hands to the warmth while cold cloaked his back. The kitchen was far warmer, yet Rosalie was in there now, and her voice, sparkling like sun-dappled water, told him she spoke of Mia.

"I think her wrist is paining her and we should make her stay in bed. She looks so tired and sad. I don't think the city agrees with her."

"It's a long journey," Ma pointed out. "And with the wreck, she's probably a bit overwrought."

Not to mention seeing him again. Or maybe that was arrogant of him to think encountering him had any effect on her at all.

He rose and returned to the kitchen. In the event Mia did come down for breakfast, he should make matters easier for her and vacate the house.

He pushed open the door in time to see Rosalie tipping a few drops of laudanum into a cup of tea. She startled at his entrance, and a few more drops splashed into the cup.

"What are you doing?" His tone was mild, his look sharp.

Rosalie shrugged. "You know Mia—unless she's changed a great deal, she'll be insisting she get up unless we make her sleep."

"Shouldn't you let her choose whether or not she wishes to be medicated?" Ayden reached for the cup.

Rosalie snatched it out of his reach. "She's in pain from her wrist. The doctor recommended a few drops, but she wouldn't let me get up for it last night."

"Ayden is right." Ma reached for a clean cup. "You shouldn't give her medicine without her knowing."

"All right. I'll ask her." Rosalie's lips turned down. "But

if she says no and then ends up dashing about town and hurting herself worse, it'll be on your head, brother."

"If she says yes," Ayden countered, "we'll know she's seriously hurt and maybe needs to see the doctor again."

And if she said no, he needed to make himself scarce.

He strode to the back door and his boots and coat. "I'm off to look for clues about that child from the wreck and his missing family, and then I'll be on the campus."

"There aren't any classes today." Ma cast him a narrow-eyed glance. "Do you plan to move into the museum while she's here?"

"That sounds wise."

Or make Miss Finney an offer of marriage before he'd intended to.

He stamped his feet into his boots. "I have some weapons to examine and oil and two students to tutor."

"You and your tutoring." Rosalie balanced a tray of tea and toast on her hip. "I'm surprised Charmaine endures it with such grace."

"Miss Finney," Ayden said, "endures everything with grace." He yanked on his coat and left the house.

He couldn't go out to the wreck yet. The sun wasn't up, and he couldn't take the horses into the cold so soon after they'd eaten. He would head up to the campus to the museum, where he kept his collection of ancient weapons. He could lose himself for hours in the work there.

Which he did. Most of the day sped by him, interrupted only by spurts of tutoring. One of his tutorees was doing so well she was unlikely to need his help much longer. The other one, a male student, needed to play less baseball and read more history.

When Ayden was about to shut the museum and head out to the wreck, his third tutoree—Liberty Judd—appeared in the museum doorway with one of the stranded passengers, who they both happened to know. Liberty was a lovely, lively young woman who showed little aptitude or interest in college, but she did show a great deal of interest in architect Gerrett Divine, the stranded passenger and a family acquaintance of hers from Chicago.

*The last thing you need, Miss Judd,* Ayden thought, *is another distraction from your schoolwork.* She wouldn't get a reprieve from distractions with Divine staying at the boardinghouse, nor at the hotel across the street.

Another guest in the house would make evading Mia that much easier. Ayden could vacate his chamber and bunk down in the attic schoolroom. "Why don't you come stay with us?" Ayden suggested to Gerrett. "We have plenty of room."

Divine accepted the invitation, and Ayden headed home to collect the sleigh to transport Gerrett's belongings. Several people had collected luggage that had survived the wreck and left it at the church. Amid the jumble of crates, boxes and portmanteaux, Ayden managed to find the trunks belonging to Mia and their other houseguests. Passengers were swarming to collect any baggage that had survived the wreck and fire. Ayden took the opportunity to ask if anyone knew of a missing child. The responses were the same as they had been the night before—no one was missing a child, nor had they heard of anyone seeking one.

He reported the bad news upon returning home with Gerrett. "It's as if someone simply dropped the child onto the train." Ayden addressed the entire assembled family and guests in the large front parlor. "No one seems to have noticed him or anyone with him."

"Did you ask about the woman with the injured leg?" Mia spoke from behind him, her voice low like cool, soothing fingers on a fevered brow.

A thrill ran up his spine. His shoulders stiffened. He

must not respond to her this way. She had betrayed him before. And she had been perfectly clear that now she was only in Hillsdale on a temporary assignment.

But everyone was looking at him, including the children in the middle of the floor.

"I'm sorry. I forgot." He turned and took in her appearance in a glance. She had always looked delicate. Now she looked fragile, as though a slight breeze would knock her over. The multitude of petticoats belling out her soft wool skirt emphasized how thin she was, far thinner than she had been when Ma had been feeding her five nights a week.

"Don't they feed you in Boston?" he asked.

Pa chuckled. Ma and Rosalie gasped.

"You're so rude," Rosalie scolded. "She's as beautiful as ever."

Mia smiled and cradled her left wrist with her other hand. "I work hard and don't have cooking as fine as Mrs. Goswell's to sustain me." She glanced at Rosalie. "And I'll be wary of younger sisters bearing gifts of food and tea in the future."

Ayden glared at his sister. "You didn't ask her about the laudanum?"

"I, um—" Rosalie bit her lip. "Well, I said it was just a drop or two."

"Rosalie, that's—"

"She meant well." Mia glided forward, her skirts rustling, her head high, though her neck seemed too thin to support so much hair. "I'm sure I needed the rest, but I would have liked to have gone looking for the boy's mother."

"He doesn't even have a name," the little girl said. "We just call him boy."

"The quality of his clothes are fine," Ma said. "I sent them out with the laundry. They were filthy."

"Did they have any initials in them?" Ayden asked.

At the same time, Mia asked, "Were they monogrammed?"

They looked at one another. Their eyes met in a flash of remembered camaraderie when they had often spoken the same thoughts.

Ayden jerked back a step. "I'm going to Charmaine's. She and her father are expecting me for dinner."

"You should stay home." Pa levered himself from his chair with the stiffness that had first appeared after his accident two years earlier. "We have that young man you invited to stay here." He started to stoop to add more logs to the fire.

Ayden strode over and crouched before the blaze to do the task instead. "I'll chop some more wood before I go."

He needed the exercise and the immediate escape from the faint whiff of lemon verbena—Mia's scent.

"The Taggart boy chopped plenty today." Pa returned to his chair and lowered himself into it with a slowness that made Ayden's back hurt to watch. "You run off if you must tonight, but tomorrow I think you should help Mia hunt for that boy's people."

"He needn't," Mia protested.

"I really should—" Ayden couldn't think of an excuse. "I should be going."

"Running off," Rosalie's taunting voice rang after Ayden all the way down the street to the Finney house.

So what if he was? A prudent man ran away from trouble. And being near Mia was trouble.

With her staying in his parents' house, he couldn't avoid coming face-to-face with Euphemia Roper. What had he been thinking when he invited her to stay there? He believed himself healed of that pain, believed offering her accommodations far more comfortable than the boarding-house was the right action. And Pa had insisted.

That was the past. Ayden was courting Charmaine Finney, and if he didn't love her with the same devotion he had given Mia, that was good, a safer course for a future here in Hillsdale. A future that could never include Mia.

He had slept fitfully. Though he'd wanted to escape the house early to avoid taking Mia to hunt for the lost child's family, she was up early with Ma. He rose from building up the dining room fire, turned, and there she stood in the open kitchen doorway. One arm balanced a tray laden with silverware and cups.

The sun hadn't yet risen, but firelight limned her face, making her skin glow and drawing red highlights from her chestnut hair. She wore it braided and wound around her head, a severe style that emphasized her delicate bones and the dark shadows beneath her green eyes.

"You should be resting." He removed the tray from her hand, his glance dropping to her bandaged wrist. "No portfolio this morning?"

She looked past his shoulder. "I don't usually eat with it."

"That's not what I recall."

A stab of pain struck him the instant he read hurt on her face.

They'd fought about that once. He wanted her full attention during a picnic, and she wanted to write down her impressions of some incident she had witnessed in town before she forgot them.

He should have known then their future together was doomed.

He should have known better now than to bring up the

subject. He should apologize. Instead, he turned toward the table. "Did all that writing pay off, or were you forced to become someone's governess?"

She didn't respond. After he deposited the tray on the table, he turned back to her only to find she had returned to the kitchen.

The room felt colder.

Seeking nothing more than warmth and food, he followed. Heat, the scent of freshly ground pepper on the potatoes and female voices swirled around him. "So what do you plan to do today?" Ma was asking.

"Work." Mia lifted slices of fried ham from the skillet and slid them onto a platter. "Rosalie should be down any minute. I'm not sure about Mrs. Herring and the children. Should I go up and wake them?"

"Let them sleep," Ayden said at the same time as his mother.

"I can keep food warm for them in the oven," Ma added. She pulled open the oven door and lifted out a sheet of biscuits. "Ayden, take this platter into the dining room."

Ayden took the platter of fried potatoes from his mother. "I'd rather fix a plate for myself and eat in here. It's warmer."

"The dining room will be warm soon enough, and there's not enough room in here." Ma pointed her spatula at the table only large enough for two. "Now take that platter in and come back for Mia's plate there."

"I can manage." Mia lifted the platter with one hand, but it tilted far enough for a slice of meat to slide onto the worktable. She set the platter down again as her face diffused with hot color. "I'm sorry. My wrist should be better in a day or two, the doctor told me."

"I'll get it." Ayden took her platter in his other hand.

"How did you hurt your wrist—hanging onto that portfolio of yours?"

"Ayden." Ma rapped his knuckles with her spatula as though he were a small boy stealing sweets. "That was unkind."

"I fell when the train wrecked." Mia fingered her wrist but looked Ayden in the eye. "But I probably wouldn't have hurt my wrist if I'd been holding onto my portfolio."

"Likely you'd have bumped your head instead, which might have—" He stopped.

The days of gentle teasing were over. After his rather unkind remark about her holding on to her portfolio, a remark about a blow on her head knocking sense into her, a remark too easily taken the wrong way, was not the right conversational gambit.

"I'm glad nothing's broken." He swung about and marched into the dining room in time to hear a giggle and whisper and the patter of small feet on the steps.

"Come on in here," he called to the children.

A boy and girl peeked around the edge of the dining room door. He hadn't paid much attention to them before. They looked about three years apart in age, but their relationship to one another was apparent in their big brown eyes and wild, black curls.

"Hungry?" Ayden asked.

They nodded.

"Is your mother coming?" he pressed.

They nodded again, then the girl whispered, "She's bringing that boy without a momma."

"I'm going to look for his momma today." Ayden pulled out a chair and bowed to the little girl. "But we all need breakfast first. Will you sit here, Miss—?" He raised an eyebrow.

"Herring," the girl said. "Ellie Herring, and this is my brother, Roy."

"Well, then, Miss and Mr. Herring, come join us." Ayden pulled out another chair. "Do you like milk?"

Ma bustled into the room, carrying a tray filled with a milk jug, glasses and a coffeepot. "Did you children wash your hands?"

They nodded and held up tiny paws.

"Good. We'll get you some help until your momma gets down."

Chattering away like a squirrel protecting its walnut tree, Rosalie entered the dining room, towing Mrs. Herring and the child without a mother. Either without or, worse, abandoned by his mother. The child was too young to say one way or another. And he was too young to tell them his name.

Fortunately, he did not seem distraught to be surrounded by strangers. When Mrs. Herring took the chair between her own children, the little boy sat on her lap, his head resting against her shoulder, his thumb poked between puckered lips.

Mia entered with a basket of biscuits and Ma motioned for Ayden to help her bring in the rest of the food. Pa and Gerrett Divine arrived in the middle of the last-minute serving, and for a quarter hour, organized chaos reigned. Once all the food rested on the table, everyone was seated and the blessing had been said, Ayden found himself seated across the breakfast table from Mia.

For months before their engagement crashed to a conclusion, he imagined this moment of having Mia across from him in the morning. The two of them would share a pot of coffee, deliberately brush fingers as they handed one another butter or jelly. They would talk about what the newspapers printed and what they needed to read, study, accomplish that day.... In his dream, they would be alone, however, and her hair would lay loose on her shoulders. She would smile at him with sleepy joy.

Seeing her with her hair wound tight, her face drawn, not joyful, and the crowd of strangers around them, his heart was pained all over again.

No longer hungry, he drained his coffee and pushed back his chair. "If I may please be excused, I'd like to get started for that baby's mother."

"I need to be doing the same." Mia looked at him then and pushed back her own chair. She set her napkin beside a plate with little food spooned onto it and barely any of it touched.

Ma frowned from one of them to the other. "Neither of you has eaten enough for going into the cold."

"I don't need much breakfast." Mia flashed her quick, warm smile at Ma.

Pa chuckled. "Or lunch or dinner by the look of you, young lady."

Her smile flashed for Pa this time. "I can't take the time to eat. I have already lost a day. Right now, I need to work."

"When don't you need to work?" The words slipped out from Ayden's lips before he could stop himself. Against the background of the children's chatter and the smell of rich food and wood smoke, that remark sounded bitter.

Mia met his gaze straight on and smiled at him, this time without the warmth. "I need to work as often as you do, Professor Goswell."

Which was why their dreams of marital bliss had been doomed from the start.

He took a deep breath to ease the tightness in his chest. "Then go get yourself some warm clothes and we'll be off."

"You don't need to escort me," Mia insisted. "I travel all over the East Coast without an escort."

"But you shouldn't." Ma's chin took on its stubborn set. "I'd say you'd be all right here, but with all these extra people in town, I'll feel more comfortable having you in Ayden's company."

"Yes, ma'am." A flash in Mia's eyes belied the humility of her response. Head bowed, she slipped from the room and vanished up the steps.

Ayden sighed. "Ma, please don't try to be a matchmaker with us. I am all but engaged to Miss Finney."

"Or that position at the college," Rosalie murmured.

"Rosalie, mind your tongue." Pa gave Ayden one of his gentle but stern looks. "The least you can do for Mia is to help her today."

"The least I can do for her—" Mindful of curious glances from Divine and Mrs. Herring, Ayden turned toward the kitchen door.

"Brother?" Rosalie called after him.

He glanced back. "Yes, sister?"

She scowled at him. "If you don't make hay when the sun shines this time, I'll never forgive you."

Ayden stalked into the kitchen. By the time he donned boots and coat, hat and gloves, Mia arrived in the kitchen with her face surrounded by white fur and that portfolio tucked beneath her arm.

He sighed. *Of course it's coming along.*

Rather like a third person on an outing for a courting couple. At least it had been that way before.

If they were still courting, or even married, apparently it would be that way again.

"Let's go." He offered her his arm.

She didn't take it until they reached the street and her feet, in boots looking far more fashionable than useful, slipped in snow packed by prior feet and sleigh runners. She clung to his forearm, her hand small and strong.

Though her wide skirt swirled around his legs with each step they took, she said nothing to him. A glance down told him she didn't even look at him. She kept her head bowed as though she prayed, or perhaps she merely watched her feet, and clutched that portfolio to her front like a shield.

"It always was, wasn't it?" he mused aloud.

She glanced up, her cheeks pink in the cold. "What?"

"That notebook of yours always was a shield between us. You cover your heart with it like you expect me to stab it."

"Or twist the knife you stuck in it eighteen months ago."

"Ouch."

She turned her head away, then stopped, a gasp forming vapor from her breath.

He followed her gaze to where the rising sun shimmered on pristine snow and icicles dripped from trees and eaves like diamond crystals. It was a sight Ayden saw so often he didn't think about its beauty. In truth, by February he'd had enough of winter for the year. Now, however, seeing it from Mia's perspective, the glory of a sunrise over snow and ice became a fresh vision, a reminder that he had once viewed the display as a promise.

He spun away. "We need to get going." He started walking without warning.

She stumbled after him, clinging harder to his arm. "And where are you dragging me?"

"You wanted to come."

"I have an editor expecting articles from me. Of course I wanted to come."

She didn't want to come because of him. Good. That was the way it needed to be. This reappearance of hers should be a one-last-time reminder to him that her desire to be a journalist was more important to her than anything they had shared.

"So you are working with a periodical?" He made himself ask the question as any former classmate might.

"I'm writing individual pieces, but if I do well with this assignment, I'll be hired as a regular reporter." Her voice sparkled like the icicles in the sunrise.

"It's what you always wanted."

They reached Main Street, and he turned toward the church. "We can begin here. No one knew anything yesterday, but things might have changed this morning."

Suddenly, Mia jerked her hand from his arm and strode away from him, her wide skirt lifting in the wind, her hood falling back as she turned her face to him quickly. "I can go in and ask. Unless you plan to go out to the wreck itself, there's no need for us to stay together."

She headed up the steps before Ayden saw what Mia must have—Charmaine and her father sweeping down the sidewalk toward them.

"Ayden." Charmaine's smile lit the morning. "You look so tired still. Did you get enough sleep last night?"

"Too little, I'm afraid." He took her gloved hand in his and bowed over it.

It was leather as soft as butter. Everything about Charmaine was soft and sweet, from her hands, to her voice, to her big blue eyes. Yes, and her heart, as well. He adored her.

He just wished he loved her.

And he wished he liked her father. Dr. Finney, in contrast to his daughter, was anything but soft. His face was etched in hard lines. His blue eyes resembled something about as soft as sapphires. Although he was in his fifties, even his physique appeared hard. Students said Finney was carved of stone, not human flesh.

Except where it came to his daughter. He smiled down at her now and patted her hand. "Would you like to invite Professor Goswell to our house for coffee and some of that cake you made? It is sure to make him feel better just from the smell."

Charmaine laughed and blushed. "Papa, you are so droll." She turned back to Ayden. "It would be lovely of you to come by. Some of the other professors are coming over for refreshment and maybe a look at that Egyptian paper someone has acquired."

"Papyrus, child." Finney sighed as he corrected his daughter.

Ayden would love to get a look at the scroll, even though medieval weaponry was his favorite type of history. And Charmaine's cakes tasted better than anyone else's in town, including the baker's.

He shook his head with regret. "I'm afraid I'll have to indulge myself with one of your cakes at another time. I have work to do to help the wreck victims."

"What sort of work?" Finney's voice rang like an ax on stone. "I know your parents saw fit to take those people into your house, but to expect you to help is not acceptable."

Ayden ground his teeth behind a plastered-on smile. "I am not expected to help. I've chosen to help."

"Is that Miss Roper I see going into the church?" Charmaine broke in a little too quickly. "I can't believe I didn't recognize the name last night. But I picked up one of my magazines after you left last night, and there was an article written by her about women going into nursing."

"Nursing is vulgar." Finney wrinkled his nose as though the idea were also noisome.

"She's proud of women who find careers of their own."

"Some careers are acceptable for females. Letters, for example, as Miss Roper has done." Finney stomped his feet. "Enough of Miss Roper. It's absurd for us to be standing here in the cold. Let's be on our way home." Another indulgent smile for his daughter. "She insisted on bringing some pastries to the church."

"That's kind of you." Ayden kept his gaze on Charmaine. "And I do apologize for turning down your kind invitation, but I have to find the mother of that little boy we took in."

Finney made a chopping gesture with his right fist. "You should bring him here to the church and let the town council find a home for him. Then you can come to our house and accomplish something more useful than associating with the train riffraff—like securing your future at the college."

# Chapter 5

As she turned to close the church door, Mia caught Dr. Finney's eyes upon her. As always, she didn't know if he approved or disapproved of her, a lady with an education and career, despite his teaching women at the college. She pursed her lips to avoid the childish impulse to stick her tongue out at him.

She had never liked Tobias Finney. She liked him even less when he took over the classics department because he was the reason Ayden had stayed behind instead of coming to Boston with her. He had invited the brilliant young scholar to join the faculty at the college until they could fill the position with someone permanent.

Now that time had come and Ayden was the frontrunner for the permanent position. Marriage to the chairman's daughter, according to Rosalie, would assure Ayden acquired his lifelong dream of becoming a history professor with steady work.

Mia shook her head from her reverie. If she didn't get her articles written, she wouldn't achieve her dream, either—becoming a journalist earning a salary instead of one paid whenever the editor chose to buy one of her articles. She would be forced to continue with her far from secure existence, making just enough money to live on however she could in a respectable manner.

The train wreck was not her assignment. It would, however, make a fine addition to the story about how Hillsdale College allowed female students to study alongside male students. Most institutions of higher education considered women incapable of learning alongside men.

"We proved them wrong." With a smug little smile puckering her lips, Mia strode into the church. Her right hand gripped a pencil. Her left balanced her open portfolio, ready for receiving notes on what she saw.

Chaos. Not as much as the night of the wreck, but still far too many people crowding the entryway and sanctuary, children crying, women looking like they wanted to weep and men with their faces a little too stony to be their natural expressions. They were stranded hours from any city of note without proper shelter, food or clothing. The room stank of wet wool, babies needing to be changed and hot soup. She wondered when these people would be able to continue along their journeys. The railroad men would have to answer that.

*Visit depot,* she scribbled in her notebook.

She began to move about, listening and jotting down snippets of dialogue. "Momma, is my doll burned up?"

"What do you expect me to do, build you a house right here and now?"

"I just want to sleep."

A hand caught at her skirt, halting Mia in her tracks. "Help me."

She looked down at an older woman perched on a low chair. "What do you need?"

"Something to eat." Rheumy eyes moved behind rimless spectacles. "I couldn't get to the line when they served the food."

"And no one's with you?" Mia's gaze strayed around the room in search of someone from the town aiding those stranded in the church.

She saw no one she recognized except for Ayden, coming through the front door with Miss Finney. The latter's smile appeared a bit stiff, and she pressed her back against the wall beside the door as Ayden carried a basket toward a table that still bore the decimated remains of toast and porridge.

Mia raised her right hand, still clutching the pencil, and waved to him, then dropped her gaze back to the diminutive old lady. "I'll get someone to help you. Were you traveling alone?"

"On my way to see my daughter in Chicago." The lady smiled, showing a fine set of china teeth. "She's having her eleventh child."

"How...prodigious of her." Mia shuddered at the notion of so many children.

"I wondered what happened to you." Ayden appeared beside her, his nearness reminding her that she hadn't always felt that way about children. Once upon a time, the mere echo of that deep, resonant voice sent shivers of anticipation down her spine of the children she and Ayden might look upon together.

But once upon a time belonged in fairy tales, which weren't real—just like their love.

She swallowed against a suddenly dry throat. "This lady hasn't eaten. Apparently getting to the food line is too difficult for her. I thought that basket might have some food in it."

"Quite a lot." Ayden crouched to be at eye level with the lady. "I have some apple fritters and muffins. Would one be enough, or would you like two?"

"Just one or the other. Thank you." Tension around the lady's eyes vanished as though she were a drawing and the artist had taken an eraser to the tightness.

"Two apiece—to tide you over." Ayden wrapped the pastries in a sheet of newsprint and handed them to the woman. "And there's the reverend bringing more coffee. Would you like some, or would you prefer tea?"

The old lady nearly turned into a puddle under Ayden's warmth. She smiled and giggled like a schoolgirl.

The corners of Mia's lips twitched. The edges of her heart twisted. She turned away and began to move through the crowd. Pitching her voice a little above the hubbub, she asked, "Does anyone know anything about a missing child?"

The tumult lowered as though someone had dropped a blanket over them.

Mia paused. "Anyone? We found a little boy on the train the other night, but his people seem to have vanished."

A chorus of denials of knowledge rose in the entryway, the fellowship room, the sanctuary. No one had seen the child or heard of anyone seeking one.

"If you do," Mia said in each room, "send them to the Goswells'."

"You're staying at the Goswells', Mia Roper?" A vaguely familiar female voice rang through the church.

Mia spun on her heel, her wide, merino skirt belling out around her. "Genevieve Perry?"

"Genevieve Perry Baker now." The smiling, petite redhead threw her arms around Mia, portfolio and pencil and all. "I never thought I'd see you here again."

"I never thought I'd be here again." Mia kissed the other woman's cheek. "You look beautiful. Is marriage to Jonathan Baker suiting you, then?"

"Quite, quite well. And you? No fiancé or even husband out there in the East?"

"No time for love." Mia stared at the muddy, water-stained floor. "I work and travel too much."

"How exciting. Did you come in on one of the trains?"

"I did." Mia nodded to her left wrist. "Sustained a relatively minor injury, but a nuisance just the same."

"A rather painful nuisance, I should think." Genevieve's vivid green eyes narrowed, and her lips bowed. "Is there any significance to your staying with the Goswells?"

"Nothing beyond the idea that God may have a rather unpleasant sense of humor, though I suppose that's blasphemous to say in a church."

"Or anywhere." Genevieve tucked her arm through Mia's and began to shepherd her toward the front door. "You must come to our house for coffee and catch me up on everything. Catch *us* up on everything. We're making gallons of soup and pounds of bread rolls for these people's lunch."

Mia smiled at her college friend and shook her head. "Not today. I have work to do." The instant the words emerged, an ache opened in her chest, a chasm in which lodged a cold, hard boulder where she had long ago tucked all her wishes for friendship, family and a home. "I'm only here on assignment."

"Ah, your journalism career." Genevieve sighed. "I thought maybe you were here to renew…" Her gaze strayed across the room to where Ayden poured coffee for a line of men and women.

Mia turned her attention to Charmaine, still positioned against the front wall like an ornamental bit of statuary. "That's over and has been for a year and a half." Her voice was cold, her heart frozen enough to hurt.

"Ah, the perfect Charmaine. If she weren't so kind, we'd all hate her."

"I don't see what's kind about standing by the door instead of helping." Mia's tone held an edge of asperity.

Genevieve laughed. "Methinks you have a few claws still extended in that direction." She slanted a look toward Ayden.

"Not in the least. I only accepted the Goswells' invitation to stay with them so others could stay at the boardinghouse. But I have no intention of renewing any sort of relationship with Ayden Goswell." She gestured around the room with the point of her pencil. "If this hadn't happened, I would have been able to avoid him."

"Avoid someone in Hillsdale?" Genevieve's tone was incredulous as she hugged Mia's arm to her rather plump side, where once she had been rather slight.

Mia gave her friend a narrow-eyed glance. No, Genevieve had not gained a great deal of weight, at least not the kind that would stay. Genevieve disguised her expectant motherhood beneath the shielding layers of woolen gown, bulky coat and oversize scarf.

"Con-congratulations." Mia's throat tightened. "I thought you were going to teach school."

"I was. I did. I find I prefer domesticity, though I do still tutor for the college." Genevieve grinned. "Can't let that education go to waste, as all the detractors of educating women say it will. Think how intelligent my children will be."

"Your children would be intelligent even if you'd never taken a class." Mia glanced around the room again, wondering if she could leave by the church's other door. She didn't want to walk past the beauteous Miss Finney.

Not that she knew where to go next. Out to the wreck would be a good idea, but she didn't want to walk all that way in the snow and alone. Ayden had been her escort, at least briefly. He had relinquished his coffee-serving duties to the wife of a science professor, a woman known for her generosity in feeding students. He was heading straight for Charmaine Finney. Miss Finney's face lit at his approach.

Mia turned her attention to Genevieve. "I think I would like to go to your house after all, if the invitation is still open."

"It is." Genevieve winked. "We'll slip out the back. Our house is almost directly behind the church."

Genevieve led Mia through the sanctuary to a narrow side door. Beyond it, a flight of steps led down to a door. The instant the first door closed behind them, the din inside the church diminished to a dull roar. Beyond the second door, the snow-clad world enveloped them in a calming hush.

"That's better." Genevieve's footfalls crunched on the ground. "Now tell me what you're doing back here if not to see the Goswells, and why haven't you written to any of us even to tell us you were coming, and what have you been doing with yourself—"

"Enough," Mia said, laughing. "One question at a time." She kicked her feet through the powdery surface snow. "I'm here on assignment for the magazine I write for. If the editor likes my article, she'll hire me as a full-time reporter."

"That's exciting. Have you been writing all along?" Genevieve unlatched the gate in a fence across the lane.

"I have. Quite a lot in periodicals in Boston and New York and even one article in a Philadelphia magazine."

*"Godey's?"* Genevieve's eyes sparkled with excitement.

Mia shook her head. "I haven't been that blessed yet. But this new magazine might end up even better than *Godey's*. We want to show women they can make other choices in their lives than being wives and mothers—marriage is not their only option."

Genevieve closed the gate behind them with a decisive click. "Being a wife and mother is a noble calling for a lady. Just as noble as being a teacher or a doctor or a telegraph operator."

"Well, of course, but some of us…" Mia trailed off.

Her gaze fixed on Genevieve's house with smoke curling from chimneys into the blue-white sky, disbursing the aroma of roasting meat. Yellow gingham curtains hung in ruffles from the kitchen windows and lace ones draped from what was likely a parlor on the other side. At one side, a trellis promised a bower of fragrant, climbing roses in the summer.

"I know this house." Her voice emerged as a mere whisper. "It's across the street from the Blameys' home."

"It is. Sadly, Professor Blamey retired and moved himself and his wife to Pittsburgh to be closer to their children." Genevieve started up the steps of the back porch but hesitated before opening the kitchen door. "No one lives there now, but there's talk Ayden intends to buy it for when he and Charmaine—that is, *if* he and Charmaine—marry."

"That," Mia said between her teeth, "would be foolish."

Because Ayden had proposed to her in the rear garden of that house during a summer barbecue.

"It's just talk. You know how this town is." Genevieve yanked open the back door.

Warmth greeted them like an enthusiastic puppy. Like a flock of birds settling in a tree at dusk, the chatter of female voices rose and fell in rapid-fire conversation. In seconds, Mia was surrounded by former classmates, new female students and a handful of women stranded in town by the train wreck. Some she knew, and some were new to her world. Either way, they were immediately her familiars. They hugged her. They fussed over her bandaged wrist, then scolded her for leaving them behind without a word of where she'd gone or what she was doing.

"You could have died in that city and none of us would have been the wiser," said a former classmate who now worked at the bank.

Mia's legs wobbled. Her eyes blurred. "A few people knew where I was."

"Like Ayden Goswell," someone called from the far side of the large kitchen.

"Yes, Ayden knew." A woman in front of her rose and pushed her chair toward Mia. "Sit. You look like you're ready to fall down."

"You should have stayed in bed." Genevieve poured a cup of coffee and set it before Mia.

"I have work to do." Mia wrapped her hands around the cup to warm them. "There's a child at the Goswells' whose mother has gone missing."

She explained about the little boy and the woman who disappeared from the train in the chaos. The ladies exclaimed and offered their prayers for the mother to be found. Talk of Ayden diverted to the wreck, then how to provide people with food and shelter, then when the tracks might be cleared and then back to why Mia had written to no one.

Mia gazed at the sea of faces around her, her college classmates, some friends for longer, from the years she lived with her now-deceased aunt in Hillsdale, remembered the camaraderie and frustrations of life they'd shared and found no useful response. "I think I was just ready to put Hillsdale behind me. I wanted to forget—"

The back door opened with a blast of frosty air. The women fell silent, all eyes going to the newcomer. All eyes except for Mia's. Some scent, some indefinable perception of mind or perhaps the prompting of her heart told her who had arrived.

"I'm sorry to interrupt, ladies, but I'm looking for Mia Rope— Ah, there you are." He strode forward and rested his hand on her shoulder. "You disappeared on me."

"You were occupied." Mia didn't look at him. His touch was enough without adding sight of him to the mixture of chills from the blast of cold from the opened door, heat from the stove and an internal ice pick working at her heart.

"Momentarily. I'm ready to head out to the wreck now. If you want to go with an escort, you'll have to say good-bye to the present company."

Mia glanced around at the circle of open, friendly and now familiar faces, sisters in scholarship and sisters in Christ, and an impression like an anchor cable urged her to stay.

"Charmaine," someone murmured.

She understood the mention of the lady. She had laid claim on Ayden, and he couldn't risk alienating her and thus her father.

As for Mia's career, its needs admonished her to get up and go with him. She might lose the opportunity for more information for her train wreck story. But her heart warned her to stay where she was—warm, safe, still free of caring too deeply for Ayden. But two good stories would guarantee her a permanent position with the journal. And she could even write a third if she also wrote about the rescued child—when she had enough to write about the rescued child, whose people seemed to have disappeared.

She shrugged Ayden's hand off her shoulder and rose. "I'll come back if I may."

"You are always welcome here." Genevieve hugged her and murmured in her ear. "You should stay."

Genevieve had said something similar a year and a half ago. But Mia had gone—and Ayden hadn't waited all that long before taking up the courtship of Charmaine Finney.

Choosing her career had been the right choice then. It was the right choice now. Her heart had survived the wound Ayden had dealt it in '54; it could survive another hour or two in his company.

# Chapter 6

She looked like the old Mia, sitting there amidst a crowd of ladies, laughing, eyes sparkling, hands moving as though she illustrated her words in the air. She belonged with these women. They were so intelligent and kind, committed to their families—and committed to education. Many times he had seen Mia in such a group, peeling potatoes or knitting while discussing Hannibal crossing the Alps on elephants, or Plato or something else of an intellectual pursuit.

For a moment, standing there with his hand on her shoulder as though he had a right to touch her, let alone act so possessively, he wanted to pull his hair and cry out, "Why couldn't you see that this is the best place in the world to live?"

Because she longed to be a journalist, and Hillsdale possessed only the smallest of newspapers. Certainly not a magazine that would print the sort of long pieces at which she excelled. Yet she could have found ways to write articles from Hillsdale. She simply hadn't wanted to try.

"I fetched the sleigh," he said with a curtness he didn't bother to disguise. "I can't keep the horses standing any longer."

"Ooh, a ride in the sleigh," the ladies chorused.

"A far cry from when we were students and not allowed to ride in a vehicle alone with a gentleman." Genevieve winked. "And of course the two of you never broke that rule."

Mia blushed and laughed, then gathered up her pocketbook and portfolio and rose. "It's been lovely to see all of you again. Perhaps—do you all think I could interview some of you for my article about women in academia working alongside men?"

"Come back any day except for tomorrow, of course." Genevieve embraced her. "We'll be meeting daily to cook, I expect, as long as the town is full of all these passengers."

"Now that you mention passengers…" Ayden watched Mia cross the room to where two women who looked to be governesses sat in a corner shelling peas. The voices of the others drowned out Mia's words, but the ladies nodded, their eyes cast down. No doubt more victims for her journalistic pen.

"Mia." His tone was sharp. "I'm leaving."

The last two words she had spoken to him until he spied her in the doorway to the train more than a year later.

*I don't care if you've reneged on your promise, Ayden Goswell. I'm leaving.* And she had.

He thought she hadn't loved him enough to stay. She accused him of not loving her enough to go.

Perhaps they were both right.

He yanked open the kitchen door, nodded goodbye to

the ladies and set his mouth in a firm line while Mia shared a few more embraces and exited the house ahead of him.

"How did you know I was here?" she asked.

"I saw you leave with Genevieve." He slipped his hand beneath her elbow. "Careful. It's slippery where people have walked."

"I'm surprised you noticed anything but your fiancée." She opened the gate before he could do the gentlemanly honors.

"Charmaine," he enunciated, "is not my fiancée."

"That's not what Rosalie says. Let's see. How did she say it?" Mia stepped onto the sleigh waiting in the alley. "'He's marrying her so he can get a permanent professorship at the college.'"

"And she's marrying Fletcher so she won't have to go to college." Ayden yanked the reins free from the fence post he used for hitching the horses in the alley and stepped into the sleigh.

Mia sat as far away from him as the seat allowed, which meant about six inches lay between them. She had set her portfolio in the gap and drew one of the fur rugs over her knees.

"You might want to pull that all the way up." He drew up a rug of his own.

The last time they'd ridden in a sleigh together, a clandestine ride at night due to the college rules about males and females alone together, they had staved off the cold by sitting close beneath the same rug.

Now the portfolio's cold leather rested between them.

"It keeps slipping down on me." She held up her left hand. "My fingers don't want to grip very well."

"Should I help you?" He looked at her, and their eyes met, held for just a moment too long.

She licked her lips and broke the contact. "No, thank you. I won't feel the cold."

Neither would he.

He gathered the reins and clucked to the horses. The bells on their harness jingled. Their hooves rang on the hard-packed snow. Hissing like wind through leaves, the sleigh runners followed in the ruts of other vehicles before them. Beyond those sounds, the world lay silent. No one wanted to be out in the cold unless necessary, and at that hour most had tucked themselves by fires to partake of their luncheon.

Between Mia and Ayden, the silence stretched to the edge of town. It expanded beyond the outskirts and into the surrounding farmland. It grew so thin after the first quarter mile that Ayden's ears began to ring.

"Do you get snow like this in Boston?" he asked out of desperation.

"Sometimes, but it doesn't last like it does here."

"I expect the ocean wind is harsh."

"The bay protects us a good bit, but nor'easters are rather harsh."

"And hurricanes?"

"Not—" She stopped as a plume of white vapor swirled in front of her face. "Ayden Goswell, when were we ever reduced to talking about the weather?"

He fixed his gaze on the sleek, gray horses. "Since you got aboard an eastbound train."

"And you didn't."

"This is my home. I had a chance to stay here and help my father."

"And I, of course, never having had the luxury of a real home, found it was wiser to go to larger, more lucrative pastures."

"You could have had a permanent home here."

"And you could have built a permanent home and professorship with me in Boston instead of the temporary position you have now."

"The position in Boston might have been temporary. You know now as well as you knew—"

"But wait," Mia continued as though he hadn't spoken, sarcasm creeping into her tone, "you *will* have a permanent position for the mere cost of a wedding ring."

Ayden reined in so fast the sleigh skewed sideways, and Mia's portfolio fell against him. He shoved it upright as he turned to glare at her. "Explain right now what you mean by that."

She smiled, but it didn't reach her eyes. They were chips of green ice. "You're the most eligible bachelor in Hillsdale. You marry Miss Charmaine Finney, and her daddy ensures you get the permanent professorship. Then Daddy gets to order you around the rest of your life."

"Who? Told? You? That?" Ayden spoke between clenched teeth to keep himself from shouting.

Mia shrugged too slowly, too dismissively. "Your sister."

"I should have known."

"And Genevieve."

His stomach sank. "What does she know of it?"

"And Rose and Marianne and—"

"Enough." He flung his hands up as though warding off blows.

Such gossip hurt like fists to the gut.

The horses began to move, flinging Ayden against the side of the sleigh. His head struck the seat back with a resounding crack, and he remained motionless while spots ceased dancing on the snow, letting the horses have their heads.

"Are you all right?" Mia took the reins from his slack hands and drew the team to a halt. "Ayden, are you hurt?

That bump sounded nasty." She leaned toward him, her face mere inches from his.

"I'm all right. Just stunned." He concentrated on ensuring the horses pulled straight and even through the runner ruts in the snow alongside the railroad tracks. "But Rosalie might not survive my wrath if she persists in talking about my courtship of Miss Finney that way."

"It's not just Rosalie."

"No one would be gossiping if it weren't for her. She's just angry because I don't like her beau."

"Why not?"

"He's an uneducated lout who talked her out of going to school." Ayden glowered at the first glimpse of the wreck by daylight.

Beside him, Mia stiffened and cradled her left wrist against her middle. "Getting on another train is going to be difficult."

"A pity you didn't find it so a year and a half ago," Ayden muttered.

"A year and a half ago you couldn't keep your word." She blinked as though clearing her eyes of tears, but her voice remained impassive.

Ayden squeezed his eyes shut against the lack of pain in her lovely face. "I never broke my word about wanting to make you my wife. I simply changed my mind about where I would teach after Pa had his accident."

"He seems quite all right now."

"He is, but he wasn't two years ago. A man needs a good, strong back to run a hardware store."

"And Dr. Goswell thinks he can move from swords to plowshares?"

Ayden grinned in appreciation of her wit. "Very nice, Mia, *mi am*—" He stopped before using the pet name he'd used so effortlessly before. *Mia, mi amore.* Mia, my love.

"I was never your love." Mia sounded weary now. "You would have come with me if I had been."

"You could have stayed."

"And done what here in Hillsdale? Write a gossip column for the weekly paper?" She jerked her face away, but her hand shot up as though she dashed away tears. "It wasn't the best writing job in Boston, but it was a beginning, and you had that teaching position waiting. We'd have done well together. Your father was nearly himself by the time we were to leave. But you broke your word to me."

"If anyone broke their word, it was you."

"You knew all along what I wanted."

"And you promised to marry me and love me forever. You could have found individual work like you do now if you'd stayed here."

"Not without the connections I have now. I had to go to have a chance at a real career in letters. But you never understood that."

"I understood that was more important to you than I was."

And after she'd gotten on that train, he had walked deep into the woods and cried like a lost child. For a year, as Pa's health improved even further, Ayden questioned the rightness of his decision. Then he met Charmaine and thought perhaps he could forget about Mia.

"You could have given us time." He spoke so softly he wasn't certain she heard.

Then she shook her head. "I had already taken money for an assignment in Boston."

"I'd already turned down the Boston position and accepted the one here." He spoke through a constricted throat.

"You made a major decision without consulting me."

Her voice remained calm, but her lower lip quivered ever so slightly.

"You could have fulfilled your dreams in other ways. That work was only—"

Mia's hand clamped on his arm. "Do. Not. Say. It." She released him as though his sleeve had turned into a flaming torch. "It wasn't great work, but it was a start. It's gotten me further, whether you like it or not. I think your family, your parents especially, would understand that."

"Arguing in front of my parents won't do." He relaxed against the sleigh seat. "I'd do anything not to upset them."

"So would I. They were the closest thing to parents I ever had."

For a moment, her indifferent mask slipped, revealing the sad, vulnerable girl who had moved to Hillsdale ten years earlier to live with an aging relative who had never had children and did not, apparently, want them. She gave Mia shelter, the occasional meal when she thought of it and little else. Apparently Mia didn't mind all that much. She had known little else in her vagabond life of being shunted from one relative to another. She knew very little of her parents, not even enough to miss them.

Unwittingly, however, the great aunt in Hillsdale had given Mia one great gift—a house full of books. Ayden's gaze strayed to a now snow-clad hillside on the far side of the railroad tracks, the place where he had first met Mia. She'd been sprawled on the grass with a book open before her. Her dress was so worn and faded its original color was impossible to guess, and the skirt was far too short for modesty. Her hair hung in tangles around her face, her skin was too brown for accepted beauty, but she looked him straight in the eye with those stunning, slanted green eyes and said, "You're Ayden Goswell, home from school in Boston, aren't you? Good. You can help me work out this bit in Greek that's giving me trouble."

She had taught herself ancient Greek because she had run out of all the English language books in her house.

Bowled over, Ayden had helped her with the translation, and they discussed Ptolemy's theories of geography and astronomy for two hours. When the sun began to set, she sprang to her feet, panic etching her features, and sprinted away, her worn skirt sailing around bare calves.

Ayden went home and told his parents they needed to find some way to get her an education. In three months, Mia was in college and Ayden was in love.

He shook his head in an effort to clear it of memories and spotted a group of men in railway uniforms raking through the burned remains of a mail car. Before he reined in, Mia scrambled over the side of the sleigh and plowed across the field of snow trampled from people and vehicles from the night of the wreck.

"Sirs? Hulloo, there. Can you help us?" She waved her pencil in the air like a flag.

Ayden reined and climbed down with more dignity. "We're in search of some information," he called.

The men glanced back and glared at them. "We aren't giving out information any more'n we already have."

"No, no, not about the wreck." Mia gave the men a smile warm enough to melt a path through the snow. "Of course we'd all like to know what went wrong, and I know accidents happen, especially on stormy nights. But what we want to know is how we can reunite a little boy and his momma. They seem to have gotten separated from one another after the crash. Can you help?"

"Not likely," one of the men growled.

"No? You look like you could." She tilted her head and opened her eyes wide.

She was going to bat her long lashes any moment now.

Ayden didn't know if he should laugh or toss her over his shoulder and haul her away before she gave these men the wrong idea about her character.

He moved closer to her, rested a possessive hand on her shoulder and addressed the men. "The little boy was wandering down the aisle when the train wrecked. Miss Roper here picked him up—"

"I was thinking perhaps a passenger list would help," she interrupted with brute force, casting him a quelling glance.

"If you want a passenger list, you'll have to get it from headquarters." The spokesman turned back to the burned-out car.

"And where is that?" Mia asked.

"Jackson." The men returned their attention to the mangled wreckage.

Mia kicked a clump of frozen snow. "Even if we send a telegram, the answer could take days to get back to us."

Ayden scanned his gaze along the line of twisted, tilted and surprisingly untouched cars. "Do you want to risk looking where you and the boy were sitting?"

"You'd do that?" She glanced up at him with her eyes gleaming and the first warm smile she'd granted him.

He'd do about anything for her at that moment.

They called thank you to the railroad men, who ignored them, then drove along the train.

Mia half turned on the sleigh seat to gaze at the wreckage. Some cars had burned when the boilers in the engine exploded. Some lay on their sides. Others tilted like weary men leaning against an invisible wall.

A shudder ran through Mia powerful enough to shake the sleigh seat. "And I was annoyed I could only get a seat in a rear car. If I'd been closer to the front—" She hugged her arms across her middle.

Ayden slipped his arm around her. He intended it for comfort. The impact of feeling her narrow shoulders in the circle of his arm felt like he'd just slammed face-first into that invisible wall. His arm shook—both with his wanting to draw her closer for comfort and for a way to erase the past hurt between them.

But Mia shrugged and slipped from beneath his hold. "I believe," she said without looking at him, "you gave up the right to touch me in August of '54." Then she leaped from the sleigh, sliding a bit on the frozen crust of the snow, and sped toward the train. "Sir, sir, wait."

Ayden hadn't noticed the man in a railway uniform until Mia called to him. He was poised in the doorway of one of the tilted cars. Unlike the other workers armed with relatively harmless rakes and picks, this man carried a gun on his hip.

## Chapter 7

At the sight of the man's gun, Mia slid to a stop, clutching her portfolio to her chest like a shield. If she hadn't been holding the notebook, she would have raised her hands in a gesture of surrender.

The railroad man dropped his hand—to the butt of his gun. "What do you folks want?"

Mia summoned her best smile. "We came to look for something in the car in which I was—"

The man cut her off with a brusque shake of his head. "No, ma'am. No one goes in the cars until they've all been searched. We won't have looting on my watch."

"We aren't looters," Mia and Ayden protested together.

Snow crunched behind Mia, and the man drew his gun from its holster. "Stay where you are, sir."

"I'm Ayden Goswell, history professor at the college." Ayden's voice was tight and too far behind Mia for her comfort.

She slid one foot back. "And I'm Euphemia Roper, a reporter for—"

"The professor I might believe, but a lady reporter?" The man threw back his head and laughed. The gun wavered. "You'll have to come up with something better than that one, missy, if you want me to let you in any of the cars. Now get going back the way you came."

"This has to do with a lost child," Mia tried again. "We're trying to find…his…people. I found him wandering—"

The gun ceased wavering. The muzzle, surely as wide as a blunderbuss barrel, pointed directly at her chest. "Get out of here, or I will—"

Snow crunched like a hundred eggshells underfoot, and Ayden's arms closed around her, dragging her backward, down beneath the bullet whining overhead like a bee out of season.

Her head on her drawn-up knees, Mia trembled and gasped and gabbled nonsense exclamations and a few prayers. Ayden crouched beside her, his hand on her head, murmuring soothing, incomprehensible words of comfort. And all the while, the echo of the shot reverberated across the snow-laden landscape and gentle hills.

"He's gone now." Ayden grasped Mia's arms and lifted her to her feet. "And we should be, as well."

"To the sheriff, I expect." While Ayden sprinted to the horses, Mia stumbled to the sleigh and collapsed onto the seat.

It rocked with the agitation of horses too well trained and old to have bolted but still restive in their traces. Mia's stomach shifted in the opposite direction, and if she'd eaten any breakfast or luncheon, she would have been sick right there in front of Ayden.

She scooped up a handful of clean, white snow and

held it to her brow. "What was that all about? Shoot loot-ers on sight?"

"Possibly, but we weren't looting. Nor did he fire until you mentioned the child." The horses calmed, and Ayden returned to the sleigh. "I don't think he actually shot at us."

"He aimed at me." Mia faced Ayden on the narrow seat. Simultaneously, he was too close and too far away. If he had slipped an arm around her then, she would have succumbed to the longing to be held and rested her head on his shoulder, where she could hear the strong, even rhythm of his heart. But closeness led to cuddling, and cud-dling led to kissing, and only a courting couple intending to wed had a right to that sort of nearness. She couldn't even hold his hand.

In that moment, with Ayden mere inches away, Mia missed him more than she ever had. They hadn't just lost their future together; they also had lost their friendship from the past.

Her eyes burned. Her lips quivered. She pressed her snowy glove to her mouth and closed her eyes to hold in the tears.

"Let's get to the sheriff." Ayden's voice was rough.

Mia tucked herself into the far corner of the sleigh and drew the lap robe to her chin despite the pain doing so brought to her left wrist. "Perhaps we should stop and tell the other workers or ask them if they know who he is."

"If he's from the railroad, I'll be surprised." Ayden's jaw looked as hard as the railroad ties. "Even a train guard wouldn't shoot without cause."

"Most criminals don't shoot without cause."

Ayden cast her a sharp glance through a veil of newly falling snow. "How would you know that?"

"I've done some reporting on crime."

"Mia, how could you? That's dangerous."

"It can also pay well." She looked past him as he turned the sleigh back the way they'd come. "The men aren't there any longer."

The burned mail car where they had been raking through the debris now lay abandoned beneath the dusting of fresh snow—snow filling in footprints around the tracks and cars.

"Frightened off like us?" Mia asked.

"Or train workers as counterfeit as the man with the gun." Ayden clucked to the horses and snapped the reins, encouraging them to increase their pace. "I'll take you home, then go on to the sheriff."

Mia stiffened. "You will do no such thing. I'm as much a witness to what happened as you are."

"Yes, but the sheriff won't take you as seriously."

"Oh, will he not?" Mia clenched her fists and gasped as pain shot through her left wrist. "Are you telling me that even with the college here filled with brilliant female students, the law officers do not take the word of a woman as seriously as the word of a man?"

"Women don't vote."

"Which also needs to be rectified. Do you know that New Jersey's original constitution gave women the right to vote if they owned property. I know there's no evidence that any of them took advantage of the priv— Stop laughing at me, Ayden Benaiah Goswell. I am completely serious. The only bad thing that came out of it was that some men realized the error and changed the wording."

"I know. I know." Ayden wiped snow and tears of mirth from his lashes. "I was the one who shared that tidbit of history with you."

"Of course you did. I forgot."

"I'm surprised. You don't seem to forget anything."

"Not as much as I'd like to."

Such as how his deep blue eyes sparkled like faceted sapphires when he laughed. Such as the richness of that laughter. Such as how much she loved the sound of his voice.

"I'm afraid my Greek is rusty. But my Italian is nearly perfect."

A mistake to mention that. Ayden had learned Italian so he could read fencing instructions in the original language of *The Code Duello*. He had said things to her in Italian that melted her insides even when she didn't know what the words meant.

"Do you still fence?" he asked, and she knew his thoughts ran along the same path as her own.

She nodded. "I've even written an article on ladies who fence."

"Dare I challenge you to a match?"

Mia squinted through the tumbling snow at the sky-line of Hillsdale and a few lights shining in the distance. "I think that would be unwise. Miss Finney's papa might not like it. Besides, I didn't bring my rapier."

"I should think your tongue will do for a weapon." Ayden sent the horses swinging onto Main Street at a faster clip than necessary. The sleigh rocked onto one runner, and someone shouted at him to have a care.

He didn't. He kept up the pace until they reached the sheriff's office. In front of the door, he leaped out and hitched the horses, then rounded the sleigh to assist Mia to the pavement. "I warned you how they'll view your word in here, so mind your tongue. I don't want you arrested for assaulting an officer with that blade you sheathe behind your teeth."

Mia laughed. She couldn't help herself. The gurgle of amusement rose from her chest and burbled from her lips. And with it, the rocky shell she built to protect her heart cracked just enough for her to see how much she had loved this man, how much she could still love him.

She tried to stuff a wad of angry memories into the breach to keep the tender feelings safely inside. "I'll be good, Professor Goswell."

"All right." He offered her his arm and led her into the office.

Heat and the odor of wet wool, old coffee and bodies not as clean as they should be filled the room. Two people steamed beside the stove, and a vaguely familiar-looking young man with curly red hair and tired blue eyes stood behind a tall desk.

Ayden's arm stiffened beneath Mia's hand. "At least he's here and not at my house," he grumbled.

The deputy glanced their way. "What do you want, Goswell? If it's about your sister—"

"It's official business," Ayden said.

"I see that." The deputy looked at Mia, and a jolt of recognition shot through her. "Catch her stealing?"

The chatter around the stove ceased.

Mia flinched and yanked her hand from Ayden's arm. She gripped her portfolio with both hands as though it were a lifeline keeping her from sliding off of a tilting deck— or, in this case, racing out the door. "I never stole a thing worth more than a penny or two, Deputy Lambert."

"I think I'm missing something here." Ayden stared from one of them to the other. "You know Fletcher Lambert?"

"Fletcher? He's Rosalie's Fletcher?" Mia felt light-headed. "I didn't know his Christian name, but we had the misfortune of meeting about eight years ago."

Lambert grinned. "She was my first arrest. Caught her stealing pencils from the stationer's shop."

"You arrested her over a pencil?" Ayden gritted his

teeth. "That does it, Lambert. A man that unkind doesn't deserve my sister."

"He was only doing his duty." Mia cast her gaze at the mud-streaked floor tiles. "I was wrong to take anything. It—snatching pencils and paper from wherever I could—was the first sin I confessed after I accepted Jesus into my heart." Her cheeks burned. "I've paid them all back since."

"But you never told me."

Mia's shoulders slumped. "I didn't want you to think ill of me."

"I wouldn't have." Ayden glanced at the people near the stove, then back to Lambert. "Never mind that now. We need to talk to the sheriff."

"He's not here. I'm the only one on station duty."

"Then may we write out a report for you to give to the sheriff?" Ayden spoke with exaggerated patience.

"Of course." Lambert removed paper, ink and pens from behind his desk. "Do you want to tell it to me, or do you wish to write it out yourself? I need to know as many specific details as possible—time, place, incident, who was involved." He paused. "What are you reporting besides that lost child?"

"A shooting." Ayden smiled.

Lambert paled. "You should have said. Is anyone hurt. Miss Roper?"

"No one is hurt," Ayden said, "but at least one person, maybe four, is impersonating a railroad worker."

Mia and Ayden wrote separate reports. When they finished, Deputy Lambert lay them out before him, reading first one, then the other, then again.

"Did the two of you plan ahead what you'd say?" He frowned at them.

They had studiously avoided talking about the incident.

"Your stories are nearly word for word the same," Lambert continued. "Very peculiar. And so is the incident. We'll send someone out there as soon as we can. Meanwhile, stay away from the train."

Ayden crossed the room and opened the door, allowing a blast of snowy wind to sweep into the station. "Mia—Miss Roper?"

Mia preceded him out the door. Ayden drew it shut behind them but not before Lambert called, "Better get that one home before the other one yanks on the bit."

"And that one needs to keep his mouth shut if he wants to continue courting my sister." Ayden yanked the reins from the hitching post.

Mia's lips twitched. "He likes baiting you, doesn't he?"

"Yes, and I swallow the hook too easily." He waited for Mia to clamber into the sleigh, then rounded the vehicle to his side. "I wish she would look elsewhere for a beau."

"Why don't you like him? He seems conscientious about his work. And isn't he likely to be sheriff one day?"

"Probably in the next election." Ayden guided the sleigh into the nearly deserted street. "And his father left him a fine house, so they will be more than comfortably off. But he encourages her to want nothing more than to be a wife and mother."

"I should think she doesn't need much encouragement along those lines. She's wonderful with the Herring children and the little boy."

"She has a fine mind she's letting go to waste."

"So where did Miss Finney attend college?" Mia gave him a sweet smile.

Ayden's jaw worked as though he ground his teeth.

"Or maybe," Mia pressed, "she doesn't have a fine mind to waste and all she needs is a pretty face and father in high places."

"The city," Ayden said between his teeth, "hasn't done your manners any good."

"You can't be shy and succeed as a lady in my line of work."

"Nor have a heart."

Mia stared at her portfolio lying on her lap, now dusted with snow. "Nor have a heart."

Ayden drew up the horses before the Goswell house. "Why did you never tell me about the pencils?"

"You mean about being a thief?" Mia's lips worked before she could continue in a calm voice. "I was afraid you would end things with me if you knew. But then you ended things with me anyway, so I may as well have told you." Her face averted from him so he couldn't see her pain, she climbed from the sleigh. "I can see myself into the house."

"Mia, I never—"

Without a backward glance, she stalked up the walk to the front door.

It opened before she reached it. Light, warmth and the aroma of baking apples and cinnamon blended with the sharp scent of snow.

"Go on in, child." Mrs. Goswell made a shooing motion at Mia, then turned to the street. "Will you be here for dinner, Ayden?"

Mia stepped into the warmth of the entryway before she heard Ayden's response. Whatever it was, it seemed not to please his mother because she closed the door with more force than necessary.

"You've snow everywhere, Mia. Go into the parlor and dry yourself at the fire before you catch a chill."

Mia glanced through the partially open parlor doorway, where Mrs. Herring and Mr. Goswell played a game of "Mansion of Happiness" at one small table, Mr. Divine bent over some drawings at another and Rosalie sat on the floor amidst a sea of children and blocks. Laughter and the squeals of excited children shimmered in the air. Everyone's faces shone with happiness or restfulness.

Mia turned toward the steps. "I think I'll go upstairs. I'm quite worn to a thread."

"You look tired, but you can't go hide. Besides, I need you." Mrs. Goswell took her elbow and steered her down the hallway toward the kitchen. "I was going to ask Rosalie to help me, but she's doing so well with the children, I'll recruit you for the job."

"I'm not much use with only one hand."

"You can stir soup and cake batter."

So she could. Mrs. Goswell set Mia at the table with a cup of hot coffee and a bowl of yellow batter before her. "Make sure that's perfectly smooth."

It already looked perfectly smooth to Mia, but she began to stir as instructed, as she, Rosalie and Mrs. Goswell had done so often in the past.

"So what happened today?" Mrs. Goswell bustled back to the bubbling pots on the stove.

"We had rather a lot of excitement. First we went to the church—"

"I wasn't talking about what you did." Mrs. Goswell waved a wooden spoon in the air as though erasing Mia's words from a chalkboard. "I'm talking about between you and my son."

"Nothing has changed from a year and a half ago." Mia stirred more vigorously. "His future is here in Hillsdale, and mine is back in Boston. End of story."

Mrs. Goswell slammed a lid onto a pot. "I'd rather my son go work for the railroad like his brother than marry to secure his future at the college."

"So Rosalie—" Mia released the spoon and raised her

hand to her burning eyes. "She was telling the truth about why he's courting Miss Finney?"

"Not entirely. I think he holds a great deal of affection for the lady. Is that mixed?"

"Yes, ma'am. Shall I—?"

"No, I'll take care of it. You come stir this soup."

While Mrs. Goswell poured the cake batter into pans, Mia stood before the glorious warmth of the stove and stirred a pot of savory chicken soup. They worked in silence. Down the hall, the doorbell rang, and Rosalie's happy cry floated back to the kitchen.

"That'll be Fletcher." Mrs. Goswell smiled. "Don't tell her, but he's going to ask her to marry him on Valentine's Day. He's already asked her father's permission."

"It should be a good match for her. Though Ayden doesn't seem to think so."

"That boy." Mrs. Goswell knocked her spoon on the side of the metal bowl. "He seems to think every female should attend college, when some feel called to another life."

"Like playing hostess to the future head of the classics department." Mia's words emerged with more bite than she intended.

Mrs. Goswell sniffed. "Hypocritical of him, isn't it? But Miss Finney is the opposite of you, which I think is the attraction. He won't have to worry about her getting notions of striking out on her own."

Mia set aside her spoon and faced Ayden's mother. "I never intended to go off on my own. I intended for him to follow me. He had an excellent teaching opportunity in Boston, and he chose to stay here for a teaching position that isn't even certain to be there at the end of the school year."

"Because of his father, you do know."

"So he says. But Mr. Goswell was up and back at the

hardware store before I departed. His father's fall was an excuse to stay, not a good r-r-reason." To her horror, Mia burst into tears.

"Oh, my dear girl." Mrs. Goswell enfolded Mia in her arms and held her like she was a child. "I've prayed for two years for him to come to that realization. But you need to see it from his perspective, as well. He hated the years he was away in the East for his advanced studies. He was afraid he wouldn't succeed out there with all those people he thought more worldly than he was—with fathers who were politicians and descended from the Mayflower settlers and all—when he enjoys mucking out stalls and shoveling snow, and his pa owns a hardware store."

"And I didn't want to stay in a town where the sheriff deputy still remembers me trying to steal pencils from the stationer's. I guess I'm right." Mia drew away from Mrs. Goswell's motherly arms and fumbled in her pocket for a handkerchief. "We didn't love one another enough to be honest about our fears or overcome them for the other person."

"I'd say you put your ambition before your love. I'm afraid Ayden—"

The kitchen door swung open. "I beg your pardon." Mr. Divine took a step back. "I left something in my coat pocket, but I can return later."

"No need. I should tidy myself before dinner." Mia scuttled past Mr. Divine.

As the kitchen door swung shut behind her, Mrs. Goswell said, "Ah, Mr. Divine, you just might be what we need to shake some sense into those two."

Mia wanted to eavesdrop, but she didn't want anyone else to emerge from the parlor and see her face blotched with tears. She could guess, however, what Mrs. Goswell was up to. For both their sakes, Mia decided she should warn Ayden his mother wasn't above matchmaking.

Fortunately, she didn't have to wait too long. A mere hour after supper, Mia stood in the kitchen icing a cake for Sunday dinner, something she found she could do with one hand, when Ayden blew through the back door on a gust of icy wind, snow crystals glowing in his dark hair and his cheeks ruddy from the cold.

He halted midstride at the sight of her. "I didn't know you were that domestic."

"I'm a rather good cook, Professor Goswell. Your mother taught me. And speaking of your mother..." Mia set down her knife. "I believe she is hatching some scheme—a scheme about us."

Ayden hung his coat on one of the pegs by the door before he responded. "She'll catch cold at any attempts there. Dr. Finney asked me tonight when I plan to offer Charmaine my hand in marriage."

"And what was your answer?" Mia picked up the knife to resume icing, discovered her hand shaking and returned the blade to the table.

"Valentine's Day makes the most sense." His hands in his pockets, Ayden propped one shoulder against the wall as though he spoke to Rosalie, not the woman whose heart he had broken. "But he reminded me there's a social on the campus that day and she'll be preoccupied with the arrangements for that and entertaining some important people at their house afterward. So I thought I'd make it official on Friday."

*Friday?* Mia's heart turned cold.

## Chapter 8

Only once before in his life did Ayden not want to go to church. That had been the Sunday after Mia left for Boston alone. He didn't want to answer the questions about where she was, see the sympathetic faces, potentially hear a sermon that would prick his conscience over his reasons for staying instead of keeping his word to Mia to go.

This Sunday morning, he knew he and Mia would face the curiosity of friends, neighbors and colleagues as to whether or not he would continue his courtship of Charmaine Finney or renew his relationship with Mia. The only way to avoid such speculation would be to suggest Mia sit with someone else instead of his family. She could. Any number of people would welcome her in their midst. But his family and his conscience wouldn't allow him to cast her off so publicly.

Mia's presence seemed to be why Dr. Finney prodded Ayden toward a commitment with his daughter when he had heretofore seemed happy with the pace of the courtship. With more men coming the following week—or whenever the track was clear for train travel—to interview for the position Ayden now held on a temporary basis, Ayden had said he would choose an appropriate time and place. Friday, while Mia was in town, seemed like a fine day, if Charmaine would be unavailable on Valentine's Day. A proposal that would surely be accepted, would once and for all lay to rest any rumors that he and Mia would renew their engagement.

It would stop Ma from trying to bring about that renewal. It would secure his future as a professor at the college, the work he'd most wanted since the college opened in his hometown.

It would stop him from wondering about what would have happened had he boarded that train east a year and a half ago.

Ayden returned from the Finney household with light steps through the powdery new snowfall. At last he would have what he wanted most—his own home established near his family and work he loved. In a few years, he would stand a good chance of becoming the head of the classics department. Life could not get much better.

Then he opened the door and saw Mia calmly icing a cake at his parents' kitchen table. Her lips were pursed and her brow furrowed as though she labored over one of her articles or essays. She glanced up at him, showing him a dusting of powdered sugar on her nose, and a mist settled between his heart and the brightness of his future. His hands fisted. The urge to slam one through the plaster wall of the kitchen surged through him. He shoved his hands into his pockets and leaned against the wall for support until his breathing slowed and his heart stopped racing. Then he told Mia of his intention to make Charmaine an offer by the end of the week.

She only smiled, inscrutable. "I wish you happiness with your hostess. She is so ornamental and well-connected, I expect an education isn't important for her."

Coup de grâce delivered, she glided from the kitchen, leaving behind a half-iced cake and the fragrance of lemons.

Ayden slammed out of the house to shovel the inch or so of new snow. Not until he returned to the warmth of the kitchen and found Ma finishing the cake icing did he realize he'd gone out without his coat.

"What did you say to her?" Ma demanded.

"I'm proposing to Charmaine on Friday." Before Ma could respond, he took the stairs to his makeshift room two at a time.

Yet one more reason not to want to go to church—he was going his own way and not taking counsel from his parents. The Bible lying on the scarred classroom table and the simple act of worship with fellow believers would surely squeeze his conscience to the screeching point.

But, the next morning, of course he went. He rose early to take care of the horses and scrape some ice from the walkways, then ate breakfast in the kitchen. Then he walked to church with the entire crowd from his house, happily darting ahead to corral the two Herring children out of the street.

"I'm sorry they're being so naughty." Mrs. Herring blushed. "They haven't been able to run around for days."

"We'll organize a sledding party." Ayden grabbed Roy Herring's arm before he could toss a snowball at his sister. "I expect the children are in need of a romp."

From the shrieks and squeals in front of the church, he spoke the truth. A game of snowball tag seemed to be in progress to the hazard of those coming to the service. One snowball came flying at Ayden's head. He ducked, and Mia cried out behind him.

He turned to see her wiping frozen crystals from her face. "I am so sorry." He reached out to pluck a chunk of snow from the fur trim of her hood, caught sight of Charmaine and her father coming up the walk and dropped his hand. "Take my muffler." He gave her the length of red wool around his neck, then strode past her to greet the Finneys.

"Would you like an arm, Miss Roper?" Gerrett Divine asked Mia. "I'll protect you."

Ayden tensed. He, not Gerrett, should have protected Mia from missiles for no other reason than she was a guest in his house. But Charmaine was there expecting him to escort her into church.

They walked behind Mia and Gerrett. Ayden listened in on the two of them chatting about something in New York City, while he had no idea what Charmaine was saying to him. Surely it was interesting. He'd never been bored in her company. She might not have a formal education past her Swiss finishing school, but she was well-read and intelligent and would have done well in academics.

Just like his sister.

Nearby, Rosalie strode arm in arm with Fletcher Lambert. He bent his head toward hers, and their soft laughter drifted through the icy air.

"Stop scowling." With a quiet laugh of her own, Charmaine elbowed his side. "They're in love. Do you think you should stand in their way with your grousing about it?"

"I wouldn't anyway."

"Don't be so sure about that. She's already turned him down once because she knows you disapprove."

Ayden stopped on the church steps to stare at her. "How do you know?"

"She told me."

"So my little sister confides in you." A little fist squeezed Ayden's heart. "She used to talk to me."

"I wouldn't say she confides in me exactly. She does not see me as a close friend or confidante. But perhaps she feels she cannot talk to you, now that you've chosen to be unreasonable."

Rosalie looked so happy. Perhaps he *was* being unreasonable.

"I'll think about changing my mind."

He began to do so right then and focused his mind on Rosalie and Fletcher so profoundly he didn't realize his place in the pew was between Charmaine and Mia.

Mia, however, didn't seem to notice him. She kept her attention either on the pastor or Gerrett Divine, sharing a hymnal and a Bible with him and keeping her shoulder turned in just enough to cut out Ayden.

He angled his shoulder away from her, as well. That was how things should remain between them throughout the service. Afterward, she would go to his parents' house and he would go to the Finneys' house.

But as soon as the service was over Charmaine insisted Mia join them for dinner. "You must tell me all about Boston. I've been to every city on the coast except for Boston and so wish to go."

*Don't accept,* he urged Mia in his thoughts.

But she agreed after only a moment's demur. "I'll be happy to tell you about Boston, and we can compare our impressions of New York and Philadelphia, too." Mia cocked her head and her slanted eyes grew positively feline, an expression Ayden knew well enough to know he should brace himself for the direct hit coming. "In return,

I think you would be a fine foil to my article about women who choose to go to college alongside men, seeing as you chose not to get an education and all."

"It wasn't really my choice." Charmaine bowed her head and peeked out through her extraordinary lashes. "My mother died and Father needed a hostess."

"So you would go to college if you could?" Mia pressed.

Ayden grasped her elbow and nudged her toward the end of the pew. "At least refrain from pursuing your career on a Sunday." He leaned toward her and murmured, "And use your razor tongue on someone who can riposte in tierce."

"Seconde."

"You're slipping, Mia. You're better off riposting in tierce and parrying in seconde."

"I prefer to parry in—"

"Don't tell me you fence, too, Miss Roper." Charmaine sounded so bored she nearly yawned.

Mia gave her a big-eyed look. "You don't fence?"

Charmaine shuddered. "Those blades of Ayden's rather terrify me."

"Have you managed to recruit any other females to learning the art?" Mia asked.

"One or two. Perhaps you should interview them."

"I'd like that." Her face lit, all signs of strain and fatigue vanishing with one flash of her warm smile. "And perhaps I can persuade Miss Finney not to be afraid of the fencing blades. They're not dangerous when handled properly. Not any more dangerous than a butcher's knife and less so than an axe."

"You are so right." Charmaine appeared to be more interested in his collection of weapons than she had any time he had mentioned it.

Leave it to one female to communicate with another.

He started to thank Mia, but she headed away from him down the aisle. "I must speak to Genevieve quickly before she leaves the church. I'm interviewing her and some others tomorrow morning." She paused. "After the interviews I'd like to find a way to get safely back to the train."

Ayden stepped into the aisle in front of her. "Not by yourself."

"Perhaps Deputy Lambert will take me when he's off duty. If Rosalie comes along—"

"I'll take you." Ayden smiled at Charmaine to assure her he wasn't abandoning her, then returned his attention to Mia. "I have classes in the morning tomorrow, but after luncheon I will take you back to the train, if the sheriff says it's safe. Now hurry with Mrs. Baker. We must not keep Dr. Finney waiting on his dinner."

At dinner, Ayden might as well not have been there for all the attention anyone paid him. Dr. Finney asked Mia innumerable questions about what she wrote. Charmaine and Mia talked about publications for ladies, about Boston culture, about getting an education versus staying at home.

"I believe the Lord calls each of us differently," Charmaine concluded. "We each have to examine our hearts and pray and see where the Lord leads us to go, whether in a career or marriage or taking care of a relative."

Ayden poised himself to kick Mia under the table if she started to argue. But the preparation was unnecessary. A thoughtful look settled over her features and she nodded.

"You make a good point." And from beneath the table, she drew out her portfolio and began to write.

"Euphemia Roper," Ayden snapped, "have you no manners?"

"Not when I need to remember something."

Charmaine and her father emitted genuine laughs, not

merely polite huffs of amusement to appease a slightly eccentric guest.

Later, while Mia assisted Charmaine in the kitchen cleaning up as best she could with one hand, Dr. Finney cast Ayden a warm smile. "She's charming and quite brilliant. If we had female professors at the college, she would be a fine asset to the staff."

"She'd think of something she wanted to write about and stop in the middle of a lecture to set it down on paper." Ayden meant to sound disparaging. Instead he spoke with all the warmth and affection he wished he didn't feel for her.

Finney's eyes narrowed. "Perhaps we should have her stay here. Your house must be bursting at the seams."

"She might like that."

And so would he.

"I'll speak to my daughter about it," Finney said. "Now, since you chose to get shot at by counterfeit railroad guards yesterday instead of coming here, would you like to see that papyrus now?"

Ayden followed the older man into his office, which reeked of pipe smoke, and lost himself in ancient history for an hour. When he emerged, leaving Finney with his scroll, the early twilight was falling and Charmaine suggested they leave before dark.

"The sky is so clear, it's going to get terribly cold for walking about." Charmaine laid her hand on Ayden's arm. "Will I see you tomorrow?"

"I don't think so." He plucked at the fold of his neck cloth to stop himself from giving in to the urge to push her hand off his arm. "I have classes on Mondays. But perhaps Tuesday? I'd like to arrange a sledding party Tuesday or Wednesday. The children need exercise and their parents need a respite. Will you help with that?"

"You know I will. Wednesday will be best."

The sledding party settled, Ayden offered Mia his arm and started for home. Neither of them spoke for the four-block walk between the Finneys' house and Ayden's. Mia clutched her portfolio as though it held all her worldly wealth, which perhaps it did, and Ayden no longer knew what to say to her. After her display in church, he expected her to continue honing her knives on Charmaine. Instead, the two of them parted on cordial, even warm, terms. Weren't they supposed to despise one another?

Apparently Mia had decided they would not. She seemed to truly no longer care whom he wed. For some reason, that notion set his molars grinding and his heart feeling like a piece of cloth must beneath a pair of shear blades.

At the back door of the house, Mia turned to him and spoke at last. "I wish I didn't like her. If she were less kind and gracious, or if she didn't have a warm heart for the Lord, I could believe you only wish to marry her to advance your career. But she is all of those things, and I think perhaps you do love her more than you think."

He wanted to believe her. He wanted to believe he loved Charmaine Finney because she was kind and intelligent and loved Jesus. He enjoyed her company. She brought him peace and had soothed his still-bruised heart after Mia had left. But the pressure her father placed upon him always lay between them.

To Dr. Finney, Ayden was the son he never had, a man-child he could bring up to follow in his academic footsteps, a male in the family to whom he could leave the fortune he had inherited and built upon. Finney would interview other candidates for the professorship, but no one at the college would consider hiring an outsider when their own director's future son-in-law was there, qualified and beloved by his students.

He stood before the kitchen stove with its banked fire still allowing some warmth to radiate into the room. *Does my decision to wed Charmaine have Your blessing, Lord? I'm still not certain my staying here had Your blessing, and I can't make that mistake again. I can't hurt another person like I did Mia.*

No answer came to him. No peace washed over him. Fatigue weighed him down like a barrel of snow. With classes in the morning, he climbed the steps to the attic, where he slept until Ma's soft knock on his door woke him in time to see to the horses, dress in his formal teaching clothes and head to campus.

After his first class, two female students approached him with tentative smiles and downcast eyes. "Professor Goswell," one of them spoke in a soft, breathy voice, "Dorothea and I would like to be interviewed by Miss Roper. Will you arrange it?"

"We promise to say only nice things about you." Dorothea Simon's voice never failed to startle Ayden; it was almost mannishly deep in comparison to her petite, blonde femininity.

He grinned at them both, not in the least fooled by their demure behavior. "You may say what you like of me to Miss Roper. I'm sure she'll be happy to talk to you two and others. How about Thursday morning in the museum, if that's all right with her?"

He then stowed his lecture notes in his office, then returned home to fetch the sleigh. Rosalie and the Herring children ran about the front lawn, rolling snow into enormous balls to form a snowman. Their cheeks glowed and their eyes sparkled. Rosalie's most of all.

She ran to him across the fluffy terrain and grabbed

his hands. "Help us get this ball atop the others or he'll be without a head."

"We're going to give him a carrot nothe." Roy gave Ayden a gap-toothed grin.

"Hey, when'd you lose that tooth?" Ayden gave the boy a playful punch on the shoulder.

"Thith morning."

"He talks funny now," Ellie said.

"Not for long." Ayden crouched to examine the head-sized lump of snow. "Let's see. I think I can lift this, but I'd like some help."

More hindrance than help, the two children got their mittened hands beneath the ball of snow and Ayden hefted it atop the stout statue. The children and Rosalie danced around with glee. Smiling, Ayden continued toward the house.

"Thank you, Ayden." Rosalie waved to him, then dashed after him. "I almost forgot. Fletcher said deputies are out at the train, so if you want to go looking, it's all right. He said they haven't found anything, but you're welcome to look in the cars that are still upright."

"Thank you. And thank Fletcher."

"Thank him yourself—" Rosalie's eyes flashed "—by being nice to him so he'll ask me to marry him."

"If that's what you want. If you're sure."

"I'm sure." Studying the dreamy softness that came over her, Ayden believed her.

She looked like he wished he felt about Charmaine.

"All right. I'll be nice to him." He kissed her chilly cheek, then entered the house.

Ma and Mrs. Herring sat at the kitchen table sorting through children's clothing and drinking coffee. The nameless little boy sat under the table stacking and knocking down a pile of blocks Ayden recognized from his childhood.

He greeted them, then asked, "Where's Mia?"

"She's in my sitting room, writing." Ma rose. "You look cold. Have some coffee, and take her some. She's been in there for hours."

"Of course she has." He accepted the coffee for himself and for Mia, then crossed the hall to the sitting room tucked between the dining room and the back of the house. It overflowed with flowered cushions, baskets of sewing and knitting, books and piles of ladies' journals. At one end Mia sat at a secretary, her bandaged left wrist cradled against her front, her right hand flying across a sheet of foolscap. She made no movement to indicate she noticed his entrance until he set the coffee directly in front of her.

"Thank you," she said, then continued to write.

"Would you like to go to the wreck?" he asked.

"Mmm." She set her pen down long enough to sip some coffee, then resumed her work.

"Fletcher says it's safe there."

"Mmm." *Scratch, scratch, scratch* went her pen.

"He doesn't think we should get shot at more than once or twice."

"Mm—what?" She dropped her pen and twisted around to face him. "What did you just say?"

Ayden grinned. "Trying to get your attention. We should leave for the wreck now so we don't lose the daylight."

"What time is it?" She glanced at a little enameled clock on the mantel, biting her lip and smoothing her right hand over her dark green wool skirt. "Goodness, time has flown. Your mother must think me shockingly rude."

"My mother knows you better than that." He touched her shoulder. He shouldn't touch her, but she looked so unsure of herself, he wanted to give her some kind of comfort. "She knows you need to work. If you want to continue, I can go alone."

"No, I want to go if we won't get shot at again."

"Not with deputies there to guard it. They should have been there all along, but with all these people in town, they've been busy keeping things calm there and thought the train safe."

"Those men were looking for something and we were intruding." She looked down, plucking invisible lint or threads or something off of her pretty dress. "They've probably already found it."

"Maybe not. We might have scared them off, too. I'll go hitch the horses." He drained his cup of coffee as he strode back through the kitchen.

"We're off."

"Be careful." Ma met his gaze and held it long enough he suspected she meant for him to be careful with more than the journey out to the wreck.

*Be careful with Mia's heart? Be careful with his own?*

Once settled in the sleigh Mia seemed bent on pretending she hadn't said anything about Charmaine the night before. She chattered in that sparkly, lively way he remembered too well, telling him about her morning's work.

"I interviewed Genevieve and a few others earlier this morning, then I started to write about the women students and what I've gleaned so far, but then words about the wreck kept intruding, so I've been writing about that instead. I think the editor will love a story about how the town has come together to help everyone who's stranded. You know, it's truly amazing. I'd forgotten how much people here care about one another."

"Unlike in the city?"

"I wouldn't say they don't care in the city. They just don't open their doors so trustingly. There are more people, so knowing who to trust is more difficult. But here… you know who are the rotten apples straightaway." She stared at the portfolio she clutched on her lap, smoothing her fingers back and forth on the battered leather cover. "I didn't realize I missed it until I found myself back here needing help."

Ayden stared at those smoothing fingers, something swelling inside his chest. "No one was particularly good to you the first four years you were here."

"People can't be good to you if you don't let them. The stationer offered to let me have all the pencils I wanted after that incident with Deputy Lambert catching me. But I wouldn't take charity from someone I'd wronged. I burned sticks in the fire and wrote with the charcoal ends instead."

"Ah, Mia." Ayden leaned his head against the back of the sleigh seat. "Is that why you're so eager to get everything you have on your own? You're still that ridiculously proud sixteen-year-old girl with more pride than sense?"

And no family left. Her aunt had died five years ago, the last living relative she knew. She was alone.

"I think," she said by way of not responding, "that's the car I was in."

Ayden reined in and leaped out first this time, dropped the reins over a tree stump and offered Mia a hand out of the car. She set her portfolio on the seat, then clambered to the ground. Together, they strode through the drifts and hollows of snow to the abandoned car.

Ayden crouched at the edge of the car. "Let me lift you in."

He did and wished she were less scrawny beneath her heavy clothes. He didn't want to worry about her taking good enough care of herself.

She hesitated in the doorway, then shook herself and led the way through the car. "I was sitting here— Ah, fifty cents." She snatched up the quarters and dropped them into her pocket.

"And a comb." Ayden fished it from beneath the seat.

They spent ten or so minutes peering under and between the seats in search of dropped objects. They would take them to the church for passengers to collect. The rack above the seats appeared picked clean of luggage. Passengers had taken it with them, good persons had collected it and taken it into town to be claimed or thieves had been at work—likely a combination of all three.

"The wounded lady was back here." Mia moved to the space in front of the car's rear door. "I think she was coming after the child when the trains collided, and when she fell, she broke her leg."

"Then how'd she get away?"

"Someone took her out the back?"

Their eyes met.

"Why?" Ayden asked.

"And without the boy." Mia grasped the upper rack with her good hand and started to step onto a seat.

Ayden grasped her waist. "What are you doing?"

She froze. "Looking more thoroughly into the rack."

"I'll do it, but I'm tall enough to see there's nothing there."

"Not so much as a postage stamp?"

"Nothing."

Mia drew away from him and dropped to the floor coated in frozen mud. "One last look beneath…the…seeeat." Her voice trailed off on a kind of squeak.

"Are you hurt?" Ayden reached for her.

She evaded him and rocked back on her heels, waving a grubby white envelope in the air. "Wedged between the seat and the wall but not fallen all the way through. Should we open it?"

Her eyes shone as though someone had lit gas lamps behind them.

Ayden took the envelope from her and turned it over. "It's not sealed." His fingers shook, and his insides vibrated. "It might be nothing more than a shopping list."

"But you don't think so." She laughed. "Your eyes are sparkling."

He felt like a child on his birthday as he pulled up the flap of the envelope and drew out a single half sheet of paper. His breath snagged in his throat, and the blood drained from his head.

"What is it, Ayden?" Mia's face paled.

Ayden handed her the paper. "It looks like a ransom note."

## Chapter 9

Mia braced her feet on the front board of the sleigh and grasped the seat with her good hand. Those precautions barely kept her from sliding onto the floor during their wild ride back to Hillsdale. When they had found no deputies around the train, Ayden seemed to throw caution to the wind and urged the horses to fly along the runner ruts in the snow. Wind whipped into Mia's face, stinging her cheeks. If she looked anything like Ayden, her face was as red as a freshly ripened strawberry. Long before they reached town, the stinging turned to numbness, and water from her eyes froze on her cheeks.

Main Street, in the middle of the afternoon, had grown too crowded for speed. Grumbling about people afraid to drive their sleighs or wagons faster than a crawl, Ayden reined in the team to match the pace of the traffic.

"Shall I take you home first?" Those were the first

words he had spoken to her since they agreed they needed to get the note to the sheriff as quickly as possible.

She glared at him. "Of course not. I'm a witness."

"But after the last encounter with Fletcher, I thought—"

"I wouldn't want to encounter any more arresting officers?" Her smile was stiff, brittle, the corners of her eyes tight. "I wasn't a habitual criminal, you know. I only attempted to steal the one time."

"Until you stole my heart." He intended the remark to tease her, make her laugh.

She wrapped her arms around her portfolio as though it protected her heart from any invasion, and she lifted her chin. "Like the pencils, I gave it back. If you no longer have it to give away, it's none of my doing. Perhaps you lost sight of it somewhere between breaking your word to me and the way you intend to fulfill your ambition through marriage." She spun away, sending her skirts swirling around her like a cloud.

Ayden reached her in two strides and slipped his hand beneath her elbow. "I thought you believe I love Charmaine Finney."

"I do. You do—with your head. That is still in excellent working condition and looking more handsome than ever. The two of you will make a fine pair at college socials and faculty dinners."

"Could we save this for the fencing floor?"

"Date and time?"

"Thursday morning on campus. I have two victims for your pen for you to meet."

"I'll be there. But right now, we need to be here." She headed for the sheriff's office.

A different group of people were milling about the stove, and a middle-aged deputy stood behind the desk. Otherwise, the office remained the same—stuffy and odorous. The deputy showed no recognition of Mia but practically bowed to Ayden.

"How may I help you, Professor?"

"We need to speak to the sheriff right away." Ayden stuffed his hands into his coat pockets, and the note crackled.

"He's busy, but I'll see if he'll give you a minute." The deputy pushed through a door behind him.

Mia arched one brow at Ayden.

"His son is in one of my classes."

"Ah. I wondered at the reverence."

"Don't be absurd." The corners of Ayden's mouth twitched.

Mia looked away, her fingers pressed to her own lips as though doing so could shove back the memory of kissing him for the first time. The corners of his mouth had twitched over something silly she'd said. Then, without warning, he'd leaned forward and—

"Professor Goswell, how may I help you?" The dull-eyed sheriff stood in the doorway to the back office.

"We need to talk in private." Ayden nodded to the watchful, listening people near the stove.

The sheriff nodded and led them into a back room with a stove, hot coffee and straight-backed chairs. Ayden introduced Mia, and the sheriff gave her a hard look. "I've heard of you, Miss Roper."

"Yes, sir. I went to the college with your son."

"Ah, yes, good of you to return to us, though no good has prompted your visit here, I expect."

"No, it's not good." Mia perched on the edge of the chair and told the chief about finding the little boy right before the wreck.

He nodded as she spoke. "Mr. Goswell told me about

it the other morning. I've put the word out here in town, but no one's come forward to claim him."

"We're here," Ayden said, "because we think we've found out why they haven't." He handed the sheriff the ransom note.

The man studied the half sheet of cheap paper with its block letters formed with what seemed to be a bit of coal because they smudged at the merest touch. Nonetheless, their message was clear. *Fifty thousand dollars if you want to see Jamie again.*

"Hmm." The sheriff laid the note on his desk and steepled his hand beneath his stubbly chin. "So how did you come across this?"

They told their stories again. The chief listened, nodded and, at the end, shook his head.

"You have no reason to believe this was tied to that child you found. After all, the ransom note was in the same train car. What good would it do there?"

"I expect whoever took him intended to mail it along the route to divert any hunters off the track," Mia suggested. "And it may be the reason someone shot at us the other day. They could have been looking for it."

The sheriff gave her a condescending smile. "That sounds like the sort of far-fetched idea a writer would come up with."

Mia stiffened. "I write true stories, sir, not fiction."

"Sir," Ayden said rather too quickly, "this does add up, you know. An abandoned child, a ransom note found in the same area, a woman who has disappeared."

"Yes, indeed, it does add up." The sheriff rose, grinning. "It adds up to a lot of melodrama for which I do not have time."

"Perhaps you should make time," Mia said through her teeth.

The sheriff's head jerked back as though she had slapped him. "Maybe I can send out some telegrams to my colleagues in other cities. But if a child had been abducted, you'd think we would have heard something, now wouldn't we, Miss Roper?"

Shoulders slumping, she nodded.

"Nonetheless…" The sheriff smiled. "I'll keep this just the same." He tucked the note into his desk, shook their hands and escorted them back into the frigid afternoon air.

"The audacity." Mia quivered with her effort not to scream in frustration. "How dare he belittle me that way. He thinks it's all nonsense because I'm a writer. I've never written an untruth in my life. I'm a serious journalist who thinks falsifying stories is unethical and—"

Ayden laid a gloved finger across her lips. "You're drawing a crowd. Let's get back to my house, and we can discuss it."

They climbed into the sleigh and drove the few blocks to the Goswell house. But once they arrived, discussing anything seemed impossible. Rosalie sat in the middle of the front parlor lining up toy soldiers for the toddler. Charmaine sat on a sofa with a child on either side of her as she read fairy tales to them, and Mrs. Goswell, along with several other middle-aged women, stirred pots on the stove, rolled out pastry dough and filled the circles of crust with meat and potatoes.

"Pasties." Mia spoke the word with awe. "I haven't had a pasty since I left here."

"Then you shouldn't have left us." Mrs. Goswell all but pushed her into a chair and set a steaming meat pie in front of her. "We're making these for the stranded passengers, so you deserve one. Did you eat lunch?"

"Not yet."

"And you barely touched any breakfast. Ayden, sit."

He poised in the doorway. "I should talk to Charmaine."

"She's occupied with the children right now." Mrs. Goswell dusted flour off the second kitchen chair. "Sit and tell us what you've been about all day."

Between bites of the succulent pastry, they told Ayden's mother and the other ladies about their hunt for the baby's family. They did not tell them about the ransom note. By silent agreement, they kept that information to themselves. No sense in alarming anyone. No sense in letting gossip spread through town and warning the kidnappers if they were still around.

Of course, they must be. Getting anywhere right now would be difficult with the snow and blocked train tracks, unless they managed to hire a sleigh or heavy wagon.

Finished with his pasty and the report of their activities, Ayden excused himself and left the kitchen. A few moments later, his compelling voice rippled from the parlor. He would be talking to Charmaine, perhaps making plans to take her out in the sleigh with no leather portfolio or past pain between them—only a bright future before them.

The meat pie dried in Mia's mouth. She took a long draft of milk to wash it down and nearly choked on the lump blocking her esophagus.

"Are you all right?" Mrs. Goswell leaned over the table and spoke in an undertone. "Do you need to lie down?"

Mia shook her head. Lying down would merely give her time alone to think of Ayden with Charmaine Finney, holding her hand, kissing her perhaps. It would only give her too much time alone to remember all the myriad details of the day that reminded her why she had fallen in love with Ayden.

She pushed back her chair. "I should do something useful like finish writing up my notes in a legible form, unless, of course, I can be of use here?"

"We're almost done." Mrs. Goswell studied Mia with her brows knitted. "You may wish to wait awhile before going into the sitting room. I banked the fire after you left, and it's likely to be pretty cold in there."

"I'll be all right."

Better off than she would be in the same room with Ayden and Charmaine.

Mia started for the door.

"Oh, wait," Mrs. Goswell called. "I also forgot to tell you that the laundry came back today, and we found embroidery inside that little boy's clothes. Probably his initials."

Mia gripped the door frame and turned back slowly. "What are they?" She posed the question in a strained whisper.

All the ladies stopped rolling and stirring to stare at her.

"It's *JMY*," Mrs. Goswell said. "Worked in fine stitching on every piece of his clothes."

*"JMY,"* Mia repeated, her blood roaring through her ears. "Jamie."

With no consideration for good manners, she flung open the kitchen door, allowing it to bang shut behind her, then raced down the hall to the parlor. "Jamie?"

Ayden looked up from the book he now read to the children, his eyes a deep, sharp blue. Charmaine raised perfectly arched golden brows in query. The two older children's mouths dropped open. Giving a start, Rosalie knocked over the row of soldiers.

"Jamie." Mia dropped to her knees on the rug. "Will you come to Aunt Mia, Jamie?"

A grin spreading across his face, the abandoned little boy from the train toddled toward Mia.

# Chapter 10

Ayden surged to his feet. "Mia, you shouldn't call him that."

"Jamie." Ignoring him, Mia crouched and held her un-injured hand out to the little boy.

He wobbled toward her on chubby legs, reaching out to her with that grin. "Momma."

She gathered him against her. "We will find her soon, little one."

"How did you ever discover his name?" Charmaine looked dubious.

"His initials." Mia held Ayden's gaze, her eyes wide and intense. "*JMY.* It's in all his clothes."

"But it could have been anything else." Rosalie stood. "Jack, Jacob, Joseph… I'm sure there's a lot more names. But you pick Jamie and it's the right one."

"It seems," Charmaine murmured, "Miss Roper has special talents."

"Not particularly. I made a guess with the *Y* and all." Mia still looked straight at Ayden, as though expecting him to say something.

Saying nothing seemed like the best course to him. Nothing about the ransom note, in any event. The fewer people who knew of the possible abduction, the better.

"Momma," the baby said again.

"That's the first thing he's said," Ellie cried.

Roy's lower lip protruded. "I hope nothing terrible happened to her."

"I don't think it has," Ayden said. "Likely that woman with the broken leg was a neglectful nursemaid, who's afraid to come forward now."

Nursemaid hired by the criminals?

"Are you all right taking care of him, Mia and Rosalie?" Ayden asked. "Neither of you has any experience with small children."

Rosalie's eyes widened. "Why wouldn't I? They've been here for days."

"Yes, but—" Ayden flicked a glance at Mia, then Jamie.

Caring for a lost child was one thing. Taking care of a kidnapped child was quite another.

Mia merely nodded and began to gather up the toy soldiers.

"We love Miss Rosie," Ellie said.

Roy gave Rosalie an adoring look. "She's tho pretty."

Everyone laughed, except for Roy, who turned pink.

"I'm getting practice for when I have my own." Rosalie grinned at her brother.

He frowned at her. "Not for at least half a decade."

"When I'm too old?"

"Ahem." Mia grimaced. "That would make you twenty-five, which is only a year older than I am."

"And rather old to be marrying and setting up your nursery," Charmaine said.

Ayden twisted his head and stared at her. Even if she weren't a mere year younger than Mia, she wasn't usually inclined to such spiteful remarks. "Charmaine, shall I walk you home? I find I need to go out again."

"Please." Charmaine rose in one fluid motion. "You'll stay to dinner with us. Your house is so crowded."

"Always stealing my brother when I want him to—" Rosalie broke off on a sigh.

Ayden narrowed his eyes. "Dinner sounds like an excellent idea if it's not interfering with something else."

"It's not." Rosalie's lips turned down. "Children, let's go see if my ma can spare some early supper for you two."

She gathered Jamie from Mia and beckoned Ellie and Roy to her, then left the parlor.

"We should be going. It's nearly dark out." Ayden rose with alacrity. He needed to get away from Mia and the sight of her holding that little boy against her. If she'd married him, they would have their own child by now, or at least—

He yanked his mind from such inappropriate thoughts and left the parlor to retrieve Charmaine's fur wrap. He intended to walk her home, then go to the sheriff again and let him know about the initials in the boy's clothes, something more the sheriff could telegraph to other lawmen. Then he'd settle in for an evening of dinner and congenial dialogue in the Finneys' peaceful household.

"Will you ask Rosalie to come to my house tomorrow?" Charmaine was saying when Ayden returned to the parlor. "She and I can finalize details for the sledding party, perhaps bake some cookies."

"I'd be happy to help if I didn't have appointments with a few of my old classmates." Mia spoke from where she still crouched on the floor, collecting toys. She and everyone else might be in danger sheltering an abducted child. One more thing to point out to the sheriff.

If the trains had been running, Ayden would have taken Jamie aboard and spirited him to some place safer. His family was open and warm, of course, and had welcomed everyone into their home. He needed to remind her to be cautious and somehow warn his family without giving anything away.

"Mia." He crouched so only she would hear.

"You're getting my coat on the floor," Charmaine protested his action.

"Mia," Ayden said, "be wary of strangers."

She straightened so fast her forehead nearly collided with his nose. "You're right. I hadn't thought of that, but— yes, no strangers."

"But what if his family comes to claim him?" Charmaine asked. "They'll be strangers."

"No one," Ayden reiterated.

Mia nodded, her mouth grim.

Charmaine's mouth was grim, too. She said nothing, not even good evening to Mia, as Ayden held her coat for her and she secured her hat atop her crown of curls. She said nothing until they reached the path shoveled through the snow for pedestrians. Then she gripped Ayden's arm hard and turned her stern expression toward him. "What, may I ask, was that all about?"

"What?"

"Don't play coy with me, Mr. Goswell. It's unattractive and you're too intelligent to play games."

He still looked at her blankly.

She sighed, forming a cloud of her breath before her face. "I'm talking about that little tête-à-tête on the floor with Miss Roper."

"It has to do with the child, but I cannot share more with you."

"I see." Charmaine bowed her head and tramped on in silence save for the crunch of their footfalls on the crust of the snow. A block from her house, she glanced up again. "I haven't objected to you running about with Miss Roper. She was virtually a member of your family for many years. You were betrothed. But, well, it does look rather bad for me. People talk in this town."

Ayden's stomach twisted. "Would you prefer I not see her any more than absolutely necessary?"

"Of course I'd rather you not see her any more than necessary or at all. She's everything you admire in a lady—beautiful and intelligent and educated."

"But not loyal. She chose a career over me."

"Ah." Charmaine's eyes widened. "So you would rather have a wife with no career ambitions of her own."

Ayden opened his mouth to say yes, then shut it again. If he said Charmaine was right, then he would stop her from pursuing her own interests, which would surely make her life—and thus her—dull. If he said she was wrong, then he sounded as though he disapproved of the life she led as little more than a fine hostess for her father and organizer of charitable events.

"I should warn you," Charmaine said, filling in the silence, "I *am* ambitious. I intend to be the first lady of the college before more than a decade or so passes."

"You expect me to be president of the college?" Ayden laughed. "Let me get hired as a permanent professor first."

"You know that is all but official already anyway."

After he proposed to her.

His stomach twisted again. "I'm not counting any chicks before I see the eggs." They reached the Finneys' house, and he paused on the stoop. "I have an errand to run, but I'll return for dinner."

"All right." Still somber, Charmaine entered the house and closed the door without looking at him again.

Feeling as though the piles of snow along walkways and drives had packed themselves into his boots, Ayden tramped to the sheriff's office. The same deputy at the counter didn't even ask his business; he immediately escorted Ayden into the back office.

"I just sent Lambert to fetch you," the sheriff greeted Ayden. "Did you meet him along the way?"

"No, but I expect he'll be happy to go to my house anyway. What's wrong?"

"Seems I owe you and Miss Roper an apology." The sheriff held up a sheet of flimsy telegraph paper. "You were right. It does seem that a child has been abducted."

"What?" Ayden snatched the telegram from the sheriff.

The message had apparently arrived only minutes before the train wreck. Its message was concise and clear. A child, James Matthew Yardley of Pittsburgh, had been taken from his home on Wednesday. Authorities were spreading the word to more and farther away places the longer the child remained missing.

"We didn't get the word until a quarter-hour ago," the sheriff explained. "Seems when the wreck happened, the telegrapher completely forgot about the telegram." He grimaced. "As though anyone could forget about something like this. Then he had so many messages dealing with the wreck and passengers that this one got lost."

Ayden opened the door to ensure no one was within listening range, then closed it and turned back to the sheriff. "The little boy staying at my family's house answers to the name Jamie."

He explained about the initials in the child's clothing and how he had responded to Mia calling him Jamie.

"Then you need to bring him to us," the sheriff declared.

"Here? The sheriff's office is going to take in a little boy? Where will you keep him? A jail cell?" Ayden couldn't keep the sarcasm from his tone.

The sheriff scowled. "I was thinking my house. He could be in danger."

"With your wife home alone?" Ayden shook his head. "Sir, he's much safer in our house. It's full of people right now."

"Mostly females."

"Would you want to tangle with my mother?"

The sheriff laughed. "She should know the danger. And don't you have other children there?"

"We do." Ayden sighed. "And your youngest deputy is there, more than I like."

"And he'll be at the house even more than you like if I agree to you keeping this boy." The sheriff tapped his fingers on his desk, then nodded. "Why don't you talk to your family and Miss Roper. If they agree, then you can move that other lady and her two children into our house so as not to cause any risk for them. When Lambert returns, I'll send him back with you."

"If it means Lambert will be around more often, I know what Rosalie will say." The corners of Ayden's mouth twitched.

Quite possibly the Lord was telling him something— perhaps that he should stop trying to manage Rosalie's heart for her.

Ayden shifted uncomfortably as he met Dr. Finney's stern eyes. Unfortunately, Charmaine's father had come home to hear the special announcement that Ayden would not be staying for dinner. While Charmaine's face showed no expression, Dr. Finney's turned the color of a plum.

"I don't appreciate you disappointing my daughter, Ayden, especially if it has anything to do with the train passengers."

"It's all right, Papa." Charmaine laid her hand on her father's arm. "If Ayden says he has something important to do this evening, he has something important to do this evening. I'll punish him by making him help bake cookies tomorrow for the sledding party on Wednesday."

"Sledding party?" Dr. Finney's brow puckered. "What sledding party?"

Ayden shot Charmaine a look of gratitude for changing the subject. "Just something I thought we and some of the students could do for the children off the train. They're restless from being shut in for days."

"Hmph. I have no authority to stop the students or you from doing something so foolish," Finney said. "But you will not attend, Charmaine. It's too undignified for a lady about to be married."

"But, Papa, I dearly love sledding." Her face turned so pink and her lower lip quivered so much Ayden sought something to make her smile.

He took her smooth, white hand between both of his. "You and I will go on a private sledding party on Saturday. Would that suit?"

"I'd love that, Ayden." She smiled. Her perfect teeth flashed and her eyes lit to a startling blue.

Her father smiled, too. "Most suitable, especially by Saturday."

When they would be engaged.

# Chapter 11

By Tuesday afternoon, Mia had heard nothing more from the sheriff, Fletcher or Ayden than the latter two had conveyed the night before—confirmation of the kidnapping. Not nearly enough action for Mia. She decided to take action of her own. It wouldn't be the first time she had investigated a probable crime after lawmen seemed too slow or altogether disinclined to do so.

Bundled in her hooded coat, boots and gloves, she told Mrs. Goswell she was going out, then tramped through the frozen slush and biting wind to the telegraph office. Inside, the depot steamed from a kettle whistling atop the stove, and the telegraph machine chattered like a collection of squirrels. At his desk, the telegrapher raised one finger to signal he would be with her in a minute without stopping his continual motion with the key. Instinctively, Mia listened to the dots and dashes coming down the wires. She had learned Morse code when writing about women telegraphers. The messages she managed to decipher sounded like frantic communications to and from passengers stranded there in Hillsdale. One or two sounded angry, a father's demand for his daughter to come home, as though she could obey without a train to carry her. Another was from a frantic wife, and a third was from a husband who seemed not to understand why his wife hadn't simply gotten on the next train.

She supposed she was as good as eavesdropping, but this was work, grist for her journalistic mill to grind down into a story. Nothing was wrong with seeking information. She didn't know names to reveal. Yet she half turned away from the telegrapher, as though she were ashamed, to pretend she was not listening to the messages.

And as her eyes scanned the room, she noticed a man in a railroad uniform tucked in a corner behind the stove and out of sight of the telegrapher. His hands were wrapped around a cup from which he sipped. Apparently he had come into the depot to warm himself. Yet something about his appearance, the tilt of his head, the way he raised the cup, struck a note of familiarity.

She took a step back, considered leaving to return at another time, but the telegrapher called to her, and running would have looked more suspicious than staying.

"I have one telegram to send to a number of people." She pulled a sheet of paper from her portfolio and laid it on the desk. "How soon can you get these out?"

"We get them out immediately, miss." The telegrapher smiled at her. "But this will cost you."

"Of course."

And worth every penny if she got good answers—or any answers. She would make the money back and then some once she sold the article.

She paid the fee. With a surreptitious glance back, she

left the depot to return to the Goswell house and her writing. The slush seemed more difficult to navigate on the walk home, the air colder. She tucked her chin into her collar and trudged on. In Boston, she would have been able to stay that way no matter how long her walk. In Hillsdale, many people called to her. Most simply greeted her. Two wanted to chat. As she paused to speak to the second person, the owner of the stationer's shop, she thought she caught sight of a railroad worker from the corner of her eye. She turned her head to get a better look, but the man vanished between two buildings.

All the way home, a brace of pencils in her hand as a friendly joke from the stationer that brought tears to her eyes, she kept glancing over her shoulder. Although she saw no more signs of anyone, she decided to tell Ayden or Fletcher about the suspicious railroad worker.

Fletcher, however, never left Rosalie's side long enough for Mia to tell him more than a brief, "Be alert," to which he responded that he always was. Alert to Rosalie's every word, yes, and distracted by her. Still, having Fletcher at the Goswell house was the wisest choice, since no one would find anything odd about his constant presence in the home of his lady.

Wednesday morning, Ayden left for the campus before Mia arose. Fletcher hadn't arrived yet, since he couldn't stay the night at the Goswell house. Who had guarded them through the night, Mia didn't know. She saw no one inside or out. She considered going to the sheriff's office, yet hesitated to do so considering that too many visits to the lawman would more greatly arouse suspicions in anyone watching the Goswell party. *If* anyone watched the Goswell party. Acting as normal as possible was surely the best tack to take.

She holed up in the sitting room instead of worrying

about vanishing railroad workers and began to write her articles. By midafternoon, she'd finished her article on the train wreck and how the town had come together afterward to help the stranded passengers. As for her articles on women students, she would finish that the next day after her meeting with the two students who requested she interview them. By Friday, when she would be set to board an eastbound train, she could send a telegram to her editor and inform the lady she was returning with three articles in hand.

By Friday, the sheriff could return the child to his family. By Friday, Ayden and Charmaine would be engaged. By Friday, Rosalie and Fletcher would be engaged. By Friday, all would be well.

All would be well with everyone except for Mia. Her work in Hillsdale would be done and she would return to Boston, her heart breaking all over again.

Maybe if she made friends, life would not be so lonely during the few hours she wasn't working. People at church were friendly enough, but being a single female making her own way in the world was difficult in Hillsdale where most females lived at home or had husbands. Her college classmates who lived there had all married. Some still worked outside their homes. Others, like Genevieve, had found ways to use their education in their homes. All seemed content with their place in life.

"I thought I was, too." Mia rubbed her right wrist with her left hand. "I'm getting everything I want."

So why did she feel like laying her head on the desk and weeping or running through the snow until she no longer possessed the strength to weep?

The answer lay before her in the neatly written pages of her article on the wreck—for eighteen months, she had kept herself too busy to remember the warmth of being part of a family, a community. In less than a week, the warmth of the Goswell family, the generosity of the towns-people and the realization that she need only be alone be-cause she chose to be had drawn her back to safety like a momma cat shooing her wandering offspring home. For the first time in a year and a half, Mia felt sheltered and loved. She hadn't felt that since Ayden told her he wasn't going to Boston after all.

Ayden didn't love her enough. He loved his career more.

Mia glanced at the neatly stacked papers on the secre-tary and smiled with a twist to her lips. *Nor did I love him enough or I would have stayed.*

For eighteen months, she had blamed Ayden for not going with her. He had blamed her. They had both been wrong, and now the damage was done. Ayden would be engaged in a day or two, and if her stories were accepted and well received, she would be offered a real place at the paper. She would no longer have to chase story after story to make a respectable living for herself. She would receive a salary. She might even be able to purchase a little house.

A week ago, that idea sounded wonderful. She could have a cat or two, grow flowers, prepare her own meals when she liked.

After coming home to a building void of other human voices with which to converse, someone with whom she could share the joys or sorrows of her day.

A knock sounded on the sitting room door, and Rosalie called, "Coming out to sled with us?"

A cottage void of someone asking her to come out and play. She hadn't played since her last summer in Michi-gan, when the Goswell family had taken her along to Lake Michigan to sail and fish in the crystal-blue water and bask in sunshine on the pure white sand.

"Yes, I'm coming." Mia set a book on the completed

article to keep it from being knocked onto the floor and scattered or damaged and opened the door to a sparkling-eyed Rosalie.

Rosalie seized her arms and hugged her. "I'm so glad you're coming. Remember the last time we went sledding?"

"Didn't we end up breaking the sled and nearly our necks on a tree?"

"And Pa forbade me to ever go sledding without Ayden again." Rosalie executed a pirouette in the middle of the hall, nearly knocking down a wall sconce with her out-stretched arms. "I wonder if he'll change his mind about that once I'm married." She sang the last word, then scampered to the steps. "Come up to our room. I've found an old skirt you can wear so you don't get your good clothes dirty or risk damaging them."

"Rosalie, you're at least three inches taller than I am." Protesting, Mia followed nonetheless.

"I haven't always been. This is old, but it's a delicious deep pink, so it will look lovely on you. Ma had it packed in lavender in the attic. I don't think she gets rid of anything."

"And a good thing that was with little Jamie here." Mia hesitated on the landing. "Will he be all right with us out sledding?"

"Fletcher says we need to carry on as though nothing unusual is going on." Rosalie laughed at Mia's start. "Of course he told me. We don't have secrets." She lifted her skirt and charged up the second flight, calling back, "I learned from Ayden that keeping secrets from one's intended is a terrible idea."

That was the crux of the gulf between Mia and Ayden—he hadn't confided in her that he didn't want to leave Hillsdale or why. That he hadn't wanted to leave didn't matter so much now than why he hadn't told her. Now she would never know.

Ayden, with Charmaine's assistance, had avoided interacting with her for two days. According to his mother, whom he kept informed of his whereabouts, when he wasn't teaching classes or tutoring students, he had been at Charmaine's house, even assisting in baking pastries to serve hungry college students and children during the sledding party.

"You are so right." Mia spoke too softly for Rosalie to hear her.

She joined Ayden's sister in the room they were sharing. Rosalie had laid out a dress with the wide, ruffled skirt style of a few years earlier. Although it was heavy cotton instead of wool, the layers of petticoats and ruffles would make it warm.

"Hurry." Rosalie danced from foot to foot as though she were ten and not nearly twenty. "Fletcher will be here to escort us in just a few minutes."

Mia began to hurry out of her pretty but practical blue wool dress with its buttons up the front. "He's going sledding with us?"

"Probably not actually sledding. He'll be there to see that nothing rough occurs. The college boys can get a bit rowdy at times. Here, let me help." Rosalie sent the folds of the pink dress billowing over Mia's head. "I'll do up the buttons for you. You are so pretty, Mia. Oh, did I tell you Charmaine isn't coming?"

Mia stiffened her face to keep her expression neutral. "Why not?"

"Her father doesn't approve." Rosalie took on an affected tone. "She may go sledding alone with Ayden after he proposes to her. Otherwise, this is too undignified."

"I see." Mia's fingers fumbled with buttons on the dress sleeves. "Then I presume Ayden isn't coming, either?"

"I hope he's coming. He has the sled. Now hurry, hurry, hurry."

By the time Fletcher Lambert rang the front bell, Mia and Rosalie were swathing themselves in hats and scarves and mittens.

The deputy glanced from one of them to the other and laughed. "I can't tell the two of you apart."

"I'm taller." Rosalie kissed his cheek.

He turned red and pretended to fend her off. "Bold wench."

She laughed. He laughed. They looked so happy Mia's insides cracked like limestone beneath a hammer's blow. The suggestion that perhaps she should stay home hovered on her lips. As though she read that thought, Rosalie grasped Mia's hand and dragged her outside.

It was a cold, clear afternoon with an inch or two of new snow from the night before, turning everything a sparkling white. The snowman Rosalie had built with the Herring children had lost his hat to a burden of snow. Mia paused to pick up the battered felt hat and place it atop the sculpture's pate. When she straightened, she caught sight of Rosalie and Fletcher stealing a quick kiss beside a massive maple tree in the front yard, and from the corner of her eye, she noticed a shadow flickering around the end of the house.

"Deputy?" she called to Lambert softly.

He jumped away from Rosalie as though she'd shouted. "Yes, ma'am?"

"It might be a trick of the light, but I believe I just saw someone sneaking around the side of the house."

Mia barely got the words out before Lambert sprinted across the snowdrifts to the front corner of the house.

There he stopped to examine the ground, then took off running.

Rosalie rolled her eyes and shrugged. "I had best get used to this sort of thing." She fixed Mia with a concerned look. "Do you think it's someone dangerous?"

"I don't know, but perhaps we should stay here." She turned toward the house.

Fletcher appeared around the house again, mopping his brow with his sleeve and scowling. "He had snowshoes. I couldn't keep up."

"Just a youth playing a trick perhaps?" Mia asked.

"I expect so, but why don't you ladies go on to the sledding alone? I'll stay here for a while and join you later."

Mia glanced at Rosalie, expecting to see disappointment or even annoyance. Instead, the younger lady was gazing at her intended with adoration. "You be careful, Fletch." She blew him a kiss, then linked arms with Mia. "Let's be on our way before everyone else is having fun except for us."

"If you're sure." Mia glanced back at the deputy tramping around the perimeter of the house. He waved her off.

"He takes his work seriously." Rosalie poked Mia in the ribs. "As you found out."

"Don't remind me of my misspent youth."

They laughed and made their way through the snow, sliding and holding one another up.

*Two are better than one; because they have a good reward for their labor. For if they fall, the one will lift up his fellow: but woe to him that is alone when he falleth; for he hath not another to help him up.*

The verses from the fourth chapter of *Ecclesiastes* ran through Mia's head. In Boston, she had acquaintances, but no one who would hold her up if she fell. If her work dried up, no one would be there to help her. If she fell ill or injured herself, no one would be there to help.

Here in Hillsdale, people cared. She had neglected them for a year and a half out of hurt and anger at the town that kept her beloved in its clutches, yet they welcomed her with all the warmth and love as had the father of the prodigal son.

All except for Ayden. He had opened his arms to another woman.

Mia's laughter died, and if Fletcher had been there with Rosalie, Mia might have gone back to the house. But he wasn't, and the shrieks and laughter from the sledding site reached them long before they rounded a curve in the road and found the familiar snow-clad hill descending before them.

And Ayden stood before them with the Herring children tucked up on the sled ready for a nudge down the gentlest part of the slope. "Hang on tight, kids."

He pushed. The runners bit, caught and carried the sled sailing down the hill to the accompaniment of shrieks of glee. Ayden ran after to help them make the climb up with the heavy wooden sled.

Halfway up the incline, he caught Mia's gaze upon him. His eyes widened, looking extraordinarily blue against the backdrop of white snow and distant pine woods. For a moment, he didn't move. For a moment, Mia didn't breathe. Beside her, Rosalie giggled, then ran forward to help little Ellie, who was struggling to manage the last yards of the hill. And then Ayden reached the top and set about repositioning the sled for another run, his back to Mia.

She expelled her breath in a sigh intended to lift the weight upon her heart. Through the vapor swirling before her face, she watched Rosalie set the children on the sled, then squeeze herself on behind.

"No need to follow us," she called to her brother. "I've got them."

They sped off down the hill, and Ayden stood a mere yard from Mia with two score or more of college students and children racing, slipping and dodging around them. Mia also saw Liberty Judd serving warm drinks near a hot fire.

"You'll want the steeper side of the hill," Ayden said to Mia.

"I'll wait for Rosalie, then." Mia backed up a step.

"She'll stay here with the children. Where's Lambert?"

"Someone went dodging around the corner of the house right before we left. He thought he should stay back and keep an eye on things."

Ayden took a step toward her, closing the distance between them so no one could overhear. "Someone after Jamie?"

Mia crossed her arms over her middle. "Possibly. He thought he should stay."

"Should I go back, too?"

Mia narrowed her eyes and compressed her lips.

Ayden grinned. "I know that look. What did I say to annoy you?"

Mia shrugged and started to turn away. But as she took her first step away, she recalled Rosalie's remark about honesty. Though Ayden was no longer her intended, she should be truthful with him because he was, after all, her brother in Christ regardless of their differences in the world.

She faced him again, her hands on her hips. "You haven't taken any interest in the child's safety for two days. Why? You've been so occupied with advancing your career— Oh, wait, I meant to say courting your lady. Why are you running back there now? Because sledding with riffraff like me and your own sister, not to mention a Judd and Divine of Chicago, aren't good enough for her?"

Ayden's head jerked back as though she'd struck him on the chin. "That was uncalled for, Euphemia Roper. Yes, Charmaine isn't here because her father thinks it's too unruly a crowd for her sensibilities, but I'm here. I happen to enjoy a rowdy crowd."

Cheeks heating, Mia ducked her head. "That will make for a difficult future with Charmaine."

"She isn't here because her father forbade it and she still lives under his roof."

Mia cocked her head to one side and gave him an oblique glance. "You think she'd be here otherwise?"

"Of course." Ayden didn't meet her gaze. "We have our own sledding outing scheduled for Saturday."

"Sans riffraff." Mia sighed and stomped her feet. "I'm either going to go join Miss Judd at the fire, or go sledding. Standing about is making me cold."

She had said all she thought she should and likely a lot more than she should have.

"Will there be a sled I can use over at the steeper hill?" she asked.

Ayden laughed. "Mia, for a lady who looks like you, you'll have no trouble finding college boys willing to push you down the hill. But if you wait, I'll use ours. The children need to go warm up. They've been here for a while."

"There's no need. I'm sure I'll enjoy myself with the college boys." She started for the other side of the hill, where the land sloped at a more precipitous angle.

The instant she reached the summit, youths surrounded her.

"We have our sixth lady," one of them cried. "Miss Roper, will you form a team with me?"

"Are we racing?" A frisson of excitement ran through Mia. "I haven't raced on a sled in years."

It had been during her last winter in Hillsdale, tucked up on a sled with Ayden.

"I was a champion here, you know."

She allowed the shouting youths and giggling girls to hustle her forward to the line of sleds poised for flight.

"Mia, wait," Ayden yelled above the tumult.

She clambered onto the end sled. A laughing youth slung himself on behind her.

"Henry Powers," Ayden bellowed, "don't—"

"Ready, set, go." The cry for start drowned out Ayden's shout.

Someone shoved them off the lip of the hill. Beaten down from hundreds of runners before them, the track lay slick as ice. No friction slowed the runners. Wind whipped Mia's face. She closed her eyes against the sting and gave herself up to the flight, the speed, the exhilaration of rocketing forward. Her companion emitted a sound like a war whoop. Mia laughed aloud, mouth open wide for the first time since she could remember. This had to go into her article somehow, these moments of sheer exuberance—

The left runner struck something solid and immovable. The sled spun sideways, backward, sideways again. Sky, sledders and trees far too close twirled by once, twice. Mia's breath snagged in her throat. Her companion and she leaned one way and then the other, trying to stop the momentum.

The back right quarter of the sled slammed into the trunk of a spruce tree. The equipage flipped over, disgorging its passengers.

Mia sprawled on the snow, too winded to move.

"Miss Roper." Her companion leaned over her, patting her cheek. "Miss Roper? Are you all right?"

"If she is, it won't be because of you." Half running, half sliding, Ayden shouldered the youth aside. "What were you thinking sledding that close to the tree line? Mia?" He knelt beside her. "Mia, can you hear me? I came as fast as I could when I saw where the sled was headed."

She tried to drag in a breath to tell him she heard him fine—along with the anger at her sledding companion and the anxiety in his words to her. His voice rang clear and strong over a few screams and too many tramping feet.

"Mia." Ayden sat cross-legged on the snow and propped her head on his knee. "Can you open your eyes?"

She managed a gasping yes but kept her eyes shut. She didn't want to observe the score of people she was sure were staring at her.

"Let her have some air." Ayden lifted her to a sitting position in the crook of his arm. "You especially, Henry. Be glad you're not in one of my classes this quarter."

"Sir, I—"

Mia waved her arm. "Don't...mad...him." Her breath came marginally easier. "I should...noticed." She dragged in a painful breath. "Truly." She opened her eyes to find the crowd tramping up the hill with the sleds and Ayden's face close enough for the warm fog of his breath to brush against her lips.

"Thank You, Jesus. You're all right. Mia, when I saw you lying there..." His face came even closer.

She closed her eyes. Her lips parted and her breath ceased again, this time due to her racing heart, the anticipation, the longing. With one more beat of her galloping pulse—

"Ayden. Ayden." Rosalie ran down the hill, slipped and slid the rest of the way on her seat. "Ayden, we've got to go home. Someone tried to take Baby Jamie."

## Chapter 12

Ayden sprinted for the house, Rosalie and Mia somewhere behind him. He needed the run, the distraction, the worry over Ma and the kidnapped baby to take his mind off of how he had come a hair's breadth from kissing Mia.

"What were you thinking?" he demanded of himself.

He hadn't been thinking. For a moment, while they sat on the snow and he cradled her in his arms, time had slipped backward and she was the woman he intended to marry, a lady he had a right to kiss on a snowy hillside.

Reaching his house, he slammed his fist onto the door handle and his shoulder into the heavy panel. It didn't budge. Of course not. It would be locked up tight.

"Ma, it's me, Ayden." He pounded his fist on the door harder than necessary. "Ma, open—"

The door swung inward and Ayden tumbled across the threshold, nearly knocking down his father. "Sorry, Pa. Is Ma all right? Is the baby all right?"

"We're all fine now." Pa rested a steadying hand on Ayden's shoulder. "They're in the kitchen with the sheriff."

Ayden headed for the kitchen, followed by Mia, a little stiff and bruised from her tumble but otherwise all right. Rosalie and Fletcher Lambert crowded into the front hall, chattering and asking questions.

Ma sat at the kitchen table with a cup of tea in front of her. Coffee sat before the sheriff, and Jamie appeared to be sleeping in a pallet of blankets as close to the stove as was safe.

Ayden stopped behind Ma's chair and grasped her shoulders. "Glad you're all right. What happened?"

"Not as much as could have." The sheriff rose as the other ladies entered. "Miss Roper saw someone lurking about, and because of that and Deputy Lambert staying here, we were ready for trouble."

"Jamie was asleep upstairs like the lamb he is," Ma said, "when somebody knocked on the door. I opened it, and there was a man in a railway uniform."

"Why did Lambert let her open the door?" Ayden glared at his future brother-in-law.

Fletcher frowned at him. "I thought it best to look like nothing was afoot."

"So wise of you." Rosalie looked at him with adoring eyes.

Ayden managed not to gag, but when he met Mia's gaze by accident, he couldn't suppress a snort of mirth.

"It was the right thing to do," the sheriff said.

"What did he say he wanted?" Ayden asked.

"He said he had orders to take charge of the child who'd lost his family." Ma wrinkled her long, thin nose. "As though I would fall for such a tale. So I told him I had no idea what he was talking about and tried to slam the door in his face."

"He slammed it right back," Lambert added.

"Are you all right, Ma?" Ayden leaned over so he could examine her face.

She smiled and pushed him away. "It bruised my shoulder a little is all. But it made me yell, and Fletcher came out of the parlor. As soon as he saw the uniform, the man took off running."

"Why was the deputy in the parlor and not behind the door or someplace closer?" Mia asked.

Ayden glanced back to see her with her portfolio balanced in the crook of her arm and her hand sending a pencil flying across the page.

"More grist for your newspaper mill?" Ayden's upper lip curled.

"Of course. People will want to read about this. Deputy?"

Lambert's face turned nearly as red as his hair. "I went into the parlor to warm my hands by the fire. It was cold in the hall."

"And quite understandable." Rosalie took one of his hands in hers and began to chafe it as though he were still cold.

Ayden cast his gaze heavenward, then turned his attention to the sheriff. "So should we move the child now?"

"For the sake of my family's safety," Pa said, "I would rather we did and let the world know so that no one tries to take him from here again."

"How will you all catch the kidnappers then?" Rosalie asked.

"We'll find them." The sheriff's lips formed a hard, thin line. "That woman with the broken leg couldn't have gotten far from here. And I agree—I'll be taking the child with me, but I won't say where I'm taking him. Best for all. I haven't even informed his parents he's safe so no one knows we know he was stol—"

Mia's gasp was nearly loud enough to be a cry. She stood with her notebook pressed to her side and her hand, still holding the pencil, pressed to her lips. Above her hand, her eyes had widened to near perfect roundness.

"What's wrong?" Ayden took a step toward her.

She flung out her hand as though to ward him off. "I sent some telegrams yesterday. I didn't think what I said was harmful, but…" She dropped her gaze, and her lower lip protruded ever so slightly.

"Mia." Ayden dropped his hands on to her shoulders. His insides felt like a clock spring wound too tightly, but he managed to keep his voice light and conversational despite an urge to shout. "To whom did you send those telegrams and what did you say?"

"I sent them to my editor and some other newspaper folk I know between here and the coast." She met his eyes. "I told my editor I rescued a child from the train, which everyone knows from our inquiries in town, and then asked the newspaper men if they knew of an abduct—"

"You sent that to journalists?" Ayden shoved his hands into his pockets. "Didn't you think how it would direct the kidnappers to us? Have you no decency but to spread his story all over the world?"

"How would the kidnappers get the telegrams?" Mia bent over her portfolio again. "If I don't spread the word, someone else will. I may as well get paid for it as well as credit for rescuing him."

Ayden stared at her as though she were a stranger as his heart compressed in his chest. "I don't know you anymore, Euphemia Roper." With a mumbled apology to the others, he strode past the sheriff and the now wakeful child and slammed out the back door.

He should go to Charmaine's. He would find peace, calm and polite dialogue there. She would welcome him without questions or accusations. Her smile would warm him, her beauty would please him and her conversation would…bore him.

No, it wouldn't bore him. It just wouldn't hold his interest when he was as distraught as he felt at that moment. He couldn't even discuss with her why he was distraught. She wouldn't understand why whatever Mia Roper did made him want to beat his fists against something unyielding.

He lit a lantern in the stable and carried it to the woodshed instead. Nothing like an hour of chopping branches into kindling and splitting logs to renew a man's sanity.

After almost an hour, Pa entered the shed behind him and removed the ax from his hand. "That's enough wood to get us through August, son. Now get inside before you catch a chill sweating out here in the cold."

"I can't go back." Ayden raised his arm to mop his brow. "If I see her with that portfolio, I just might toss it into the fire."

"Why?"

"Why?" Ayden faced his father, his eyes wide. "Pa, she has no sense of decency any longer. She's writing about the train wreck and all the suffering there."

"She wrote about how this town came together to help one another in true Christian charity."

"She's writing about how women are treated in their classes, likely looking for ways they are slighted—"

"She's writing about how much women are respected for their intelligence and ability to learn."

"And how all the professors are male."

"And how one of the professors takes his own time to tutor students at risk of failing."

"And now to make a spectacle of that unfortunate child and his family, giving them no peace—"

"You don't know that." Pa jabbed a finger into Ayden's chest. "You're making unfair assumptions about that lovely young woman, just like you did eighteen months ago, and you're not the only one who will be hurt over it this time." He cleared his throat and looked away. "You weren't the only one hurt last time. Your Ma and I love her like a daughter, and you took her away from us."

"I took her away from you?" Ayden pressed his arms across his chest. "I was the one who stayed to help you all."

"Is that why you stayed?" Pa propped a shoulder against the woodshed doorway. "You're a grown man and have to make your own mistakes. But I was perfectly capable of continuing my work at the store by the time you chose to stay. You are a loyal son, but that was a poor excuse at best. You were afraid to go east—"

"Of course I wasn't afraid to go east. I studied there for four years. I was asked to return. I didn't apply."

"Then why didn't you go when Mia made it clear she would?"

The heat from his exertions dissipating, cold began to seep deep into Ayden. Bone deep. Heart deep. Soul deep.

He yanked his coat from a peg and threw it around his shoulders. "It doesn't matter now. She chose to leave me, and I've chosen someone else."

Pa's shoulders slumped. "For the right reasons?"

"Of course." But Ayden couldn't meet his father's eyes.

Pa rested his hand on Ayden's shoulder again. "If you're certain you are in the Lord's will in your future and not your own, then your mother and I will accept it. Now come inside and get warmed up." He turned and left the shed.

Ayden followed, his footfalls dragging just a little. He didn't want to see Mia. He probably owed her an apology.

He had made judgments about her work without reading it first. But her sending telegrams was careless at best. Just like he'd been, not letting her know all that had transpired with Baby Jamie.

Seeing a light shining beneath the sitting room door, he knocked, then opened it. Mia sat before the fire still in that pretty pink dress that looked vaguely familiar to him. She wore no shoes, only her white lisle stockings, and her hair hung down her back in a single braid, her pins lying in a neat pile on the table beside her.

She glanced up at him and hugged a sheaf of papers against her as though she thought he might steal them away. "Did you find the supper your mother left warming in the oven?"

"Not yet." He closed the door and approached the fire. As its warmth hit him, he began to shiver from the cold. "I can bring you more wood." He gave her a rueful smile. "I chopped enough."

"No need. I just wanted to finish making notes on this article, and then I'm off to bed. I have a lot of work to do tomorrow." She looked away and drew her stockinged toes beneath the hem of her dress. "Unless you won't take me to campus."

"I said I would."

"You've said a number of things you would do." She smacked the palm of her hand against her manuscript. "This is too long. I just can't work out what to leave out. I have heard so many stories and seen so much during and since the wreck."

Ayden smiled. "I wish I had you for a student. Most don't have enough to say about anything. I give them a topic like the War of the Roses, and they say they didn't have enough information to write a twenty-page paper."

They exchanged polite, stiff smiles.

Ayden crouched closer to the fire, absorbing more of its warmth. "Why don't you write a book about the wreck?"

"I don't think I have enough material for a book. Perhaps two or three articles."

"A novel?"

She laughed. "I am not Charlotte Brontë, as much as I wish I were."

"If you wish it, why don't you do it?"

Mia shrugged. "No time. I am always looking for the next story to write and sell."

"You seem to be doing well."

"I am for a lady journalist. But this salaried position will be less taxing."

"I expect so." Ayden shifted so he faced her. "I'm sorry about earlier."

"You were concerned about your family's safety with reason. I...well, I sent those telegrams no matter how important the story. I didn't think the kidnappers would spy on the telegraph."

"Have you heard anything back?"

She shook her head. "I'm beginning to think they intercepted any return messages."

"It was a foolish thing to do, you know."

"Why? They hadn't come here before today and we've talked about the boy all over town."

"The house was full of people until this afternoon, making it much harder to manage another abduction."

"Leave it to a war historian to think of tactics," Mia muttered. She rubbed her eyes. "I just want this story so badly. It's exclusive and—"

"Potentially dangerous." Ayden touched her cheek, her skin as smooth as fire-warmed silk. "Everything is fine now. The child's been moved, the parents have been notified and he will go home on Friday, all because you helped him on the train."

"What else would I do? No one else seemed inclined to do any good beyond saving themselves."

Of course not, except for Mia with her kind and generous heart.

His conscience jabbed him like a foil without its button tip and he flicked his gaze to her papers. "I'm also sorry about the things I've been thinking and saying about your work. I shouldn't have criticized it without reading it."

"Thank you for that. I try not to be a vulture feeding off others' pain. I strive to educate and inform. I want this article about the college to encourage other young women to get an education. Even if they get married and choose to focus on their family, not on having a career, an education never goes amiss. What if they end up moving to the frontier? They can educate their children well and even educate the children of others well." Her eyes sparkled like polished jade. "One thing I've learned while here talking to the women who graduated with me, and even before me, is that an education is never wasted."

"No, it's not."

It was what he tried to tell her a year and a half earlier when she accused him of wanting her to throw away her education for a life with no future. His future was to have been with her, his helpmeet, his wife, the mother to his children and an intellectual equal who could keep his thinking clear and mental faculties sharpened no matter what he did.

And what she wanted to do didn't matter because it was all for him.

What a selfish, thoughtless man he'd been. Eighteen months earlier, he had cast a die he couldn't now break because he had acted upon his will without seeking after the Lord's.

Feeling as though someone had stacked upon his shoulders all the wood he'd chopped, he rose. "I'd like to read your article about the college if you'll let me."

"Of course." She smiled at him, not quite the heart-melting smile that tilted up the corners of her eyes, but neither was it the frosty, polite one she'd been giving him all week. "I only say nice things about the youngest history professor."

"Will you still say nice things after our fencing match tomorrow?"

"Only if I win." The smile warmed a degree or two.

"We'll leave here at eight o'clock, then." He reached out his hand. They shook on the bargain, and he left the room looking forward to fencing with Mia on Thursday morning far more than making an offer of marriage to Charmaine on Friday.

# Chapter 13

"*En garde. Prêt. Allez.*" One of Ayden's male students gave the call. Mia and Ayden saluted one another with their blades, then engaged. Ayden's right foot came down heel to toe and his blade shot forward in a lunge—as Mia knew it would. Smiling, she feinted, then raised her blade in *quarte* as though she intended to protect the upper left part of her torso. A second before the foil of his blade touched hers, she countered, circling her rapier to the right and down.

"Nice *octave*." Ayden smiled back. "A pity you're too slow." His blade tip caught the forte of Mia's blade near the hilt, knocking her rapier out of position.

She disengaged and retreated, then lunged fast enough to tap her buttoned tip on his chest. The student spectators gasped.

Mia laughed. "Too slow, am I?"

She attacked in *sixte*. Ayden was ready for her with his blade in *quarte*. The foils rang together. A *remise* of parries and ripostes, lunges and retreats began. Their blades flashed like silver lightning. The foil ends rang together like chimes. The forte ends near the hilt crashed like cymbals. It was a game of speed and endurance Mia doubted she could win. Her right arm ached. Her breath rasped in her throat, and she was forming a most unladylike dew on her brow.

"Ready to give up?" Ayden taunted.

"No." Even if she was.

"City's made you weak."

"Being a professor has made you boorish."

The students laughed. Ayden's gaze flicked their way for a second. Only a second. Enough time. Mia sent her blade singing down Ayden's in a *glissade,* caught her forte on his and, with an upward jerk of her arm, sent his rapier spinning through the air.

The students applauded.

Ayden's empty right hand dropped to his side. His lips parted, then he shook his head. "I can't remember the last time anyone disarmed me."

"August 10, 1854." Mia smiled, though her heart constricted.

She had been happy then, certain the world was hers to conquer and own with Ayden at her side.

"You might be right." He retrieved his blade and glared at his students. "Not a word out of any of you."

"No, sir." They chorused like reciting children in a grammar school.

Then they dispersed, snickering behind their hands.

"I'm undone." Ayden grinned. "That little move of yours will be all over the campus before I get to class."

"You should have remembered it. I remembered all of yours." She switched her borrowed rapier to her left hand

and held out her right. "It was only because I have fenced with you so often I got anywhere near under your guard."

Ayden took her hand, shook it and kept holding it. "You've gotten under my guard all right."

The way he held her gaze along with her hand told Mia he meant far more than her trick with the blade. In a moment, he would have gotten under her guard, and she would be undone to her soul.

She drew her hand free. "I have interviews to conduct and you have a class to lead. But thank you for the match. The last time I fenced was about six months ago, when I wrote a story about a group of lady fencers. They made me have a bout with one of their champions before they would agree to be interviewed."

"Did you win?"

"I got the story."

"And an invitation to join?"

Mia snorted. "I said lady fencers. I am not considered to be much of a lady. I earn my living."

"Euphemia Roper, you could scrub floors for a living and still be a lady." Abruptly Ayden turned away and snatched up his coat. "I'd better lock these blades up and get to class." He kept his back to her. "And because you humiliated me in front of my students, I think you should pay me back by helping Miss Judd with her essay."

In truth, she should interview the students, then leave the campus. She wouldn't see him the rest of the day. Likely, the next time she would see him, he would be engaged to Charmaine Finney, his decision made to, once again, choose his career over her.

As she had done to him.

"What time?" she asked.

He told her. She sought for an excuse to say no. Nothing truthful came to mind.

"All right." She gathered her coat and headed upstairs to meet the students.

Two young women had turned into four ladies and six young men, two of whom she had met through Genevieve earlier and one of whom had been her partner on their ill-fated sledding race.

Time sped by as she took notes, asked questions and answered even more. They carried her off to eat luncheon with them, and when she returned to the lobby, Ayden stood in the middle of the room talking to Mr. Divine and Miss Judd.

He waved to Mia. "Just in time. Gerrett and I are going to help Miss Judd by giving her a match—unless you'll allow me to get my revenge." He grinned. His blue eyes sparkled.

And Mia's heart broke free of its protective shell and tumbled at his feet.

Hours later, her feet half frozen from tramping through slush, her cheeks stiff from the dried tears on her face, Mia trudged up to the Goswell house. If she was fortunate, Mrs. Goswell would be somewhere other than the kitchen—like out shopping—and she could avoid her. She hoped she could avoid everyone—at least until the trains started running and she could escape from Hillsdale and all its memories, both old and new.

Instinct had warned her to run the moment she realized she was still desperately in love with Ayden. Instead, she'd stayed and helped Miss Judd with her understanding of the art of fencing.

Mia pushed open the kitchen door and found Mrs. Goswell applying strawberry jam in the shape of a heart to the center of a cake. Her dreams of escape were dashed.

"Fresh strawberries would be much nicer, but none

of the hothouse variety have gotten through yet with the trains not running."

"It's very pretty just the same." Mia spoke the truth without enthusiasm. "Is that for Rosalie and Deputy Lambert? Or is it for you and Mr. Goswell?"

Mrs. Goswell laughed. "It's for everyone. It's a spice cake, and I prefer brown sugar icing with it, but that doesn't look as pretty with the white sugar icing and the red."

"It smells wonderful." The medley of nutmeg and cinnamon, blended with the aroma of a roast in the oven, tantalized Mia's knotted stomach.

"Let's hope it tastes as wonderful as it smells." Mrs. Goswell set down her knife. "Now, did you have anything to— Dear me, what's wrong?"

"Wrong?" Mia kept her face averted. "I'm tired and cold."

"I'm sure that's true, but you have also been crying. Why?"

Mia compressed her lips in an effort to keep them from quivering. Her eyes filled, and she squeezed them shut to stop tears from spilling out. Instead, the action sent tears sliding down her cheeks atop their dried companions.

She dashed them away with her gloves. "Excuse me." She tried to glide past Ayden's mother.

Mrs. Goswell blocked her way. "I was the closest thing to a mother you had for four years. I fed you into looking like a female instead of a bean pole. I taught you how to cook and dress right and talk like a lady. I even told my son letting you go was the stupidest thing he ever did. I think that gives me the right to know why you are so unhappy."

"A week ago, I would have told you that nothing I do is any of your business. But that was before I was back here and reminded that people here care about me...." Mia dropped onto a kitchen chair and dropped her head onto her folded arms. "I disarmed him this morning in front of his students."

"You're crying about that?" Mrs. Goswell laughed. "It's about time someone got the best of him. You'll be a legend here."

"I tried to help one of his female students with an assignment."

"Miss Short or Miss Judd?"

"Miss Judd. She gives up too easily, and I told her she was a coward who wouldn't even fight for love."

"Hmm." Mrs. Goswell drew out the other chair and sat. "Do you have reason to know this?"

Mia lifted her head. "It's embarrassingly obvious she's in love with Mr. Divine."

"I noticed that at church on Sunday. But why did that make you cry?"

"I told her she was just like Ayden, afraid to fight even for love."

A gleam brightened Mrs. Goswell's light blue eyes. "Did he hear you?"

"I'm certain he did." Mia dug in her pocket for a handkerchief and wiped her eyes. "But I was wrong. At least, I was the pot calling the kettle black. I was the one who wasn't willing to fight for my love. And I still love him and now it's too late." The last emerged as a wail like she hadn't uttered in front of another person since she was a child, if she had ever done it then.

And Mrs. Goswell just smiled. "It's about time you admitted it."

"It doesn't matter if I do. He's going to marry Charmaine Finney so he can stay here forever."

"Has he offered for her yet?"

"No, but he will because if he doesn't his position at the college will end with the quarter."

"As if my brilliant son couldn't get work elsewhere."

"He doesn't want to go elsewhere. He wants to stay where people love him and respect him and he can do things professors aren't supposed to do like muck out stalls and chop wood." Mia wrinkled her nose. "And my work is in Boston. Nothing has changed in a year and a half."

"Apparently not." Mrs. Goswell stood and resumed decorating the cake. "You prefer your career to love and community, and he prefers his career to love and friendship. And have either of you ever asked the Lord what He wants for you?"

Mia curled her fingers around the edge of the table and gnawed on the inside of her lower lip. Finally, she shook her head. "I thought I was doing what the Lord wanted for me. And that included leaving Ayden behind. If writing articles in the East isn't what the Lord wants for me, why has He made it all possible?"

"Temptation comes in the guise of the easy road or the road we think we want."

"Losing Ayden wasn't easy."

"Nor will getting him back be easy. You have choices to make."

Mia rose. "I can't make them if he is determined to marry Charmaine to ensure his future position at the college."

"Mia, I will do what I can to help. The rest is up to you and Ayden and the Lord." Mrs. Goswell squeezed Mia's hand. "Now go put on that pretty blue dress you wore to church and my husband will take you up to the social."

"No, thank you. I'd rather stay here and finish my articles."

"All right. Then put on that pretty blue dress for supper. Everyone will be here. And that means Ayden."

She couldn't avoid dinner with the family. That would

be unforgivably rude after Mrs. Goswell was taking so much trouble. She would wear the one formal dress she had brought with her and perhaps wear her hair in a less severe style. Somehow she would get through an evening with Ayden across the table from her.

And after that…she would lose herself in her work and not think about Ayden. It had gotten her through those first months alone in the city. It would get her through more painful months ahead…and the rest of her life.

She washed her face, accepted a cup of coffee from Mrs. Goswell and escaped into the sitting room. Her manuscript lay undisturbed beneath the stack of books she'd set atop it, and she plunged into editing the entire article, rephrasing and moving one paragraph to another page, removing a few lines and adding others. By the time Mrs. Goswell knocked on the door to remind her to get ready for dinner, the article about women at college was finished. It was time to begin the story of the abducted little boy ending up on one of the wrecked trains. If anything would cement her standing as a journalist, this article would. Even when the story became public and other journalists wrote about it, she would still be the reporter who had carried him from the train and first documented it.

If only she knew where the sheriff had taken him. With the boy spirited away, she didn't know how to end the story. With God's grace, Jamie would be returned to his family once the trains were running again or the snow melted enough to clear the roads. But when? And how?

Back and fingers stiff from working too long without replenishing the fire, Mia tucked her partially written manuscript beneath the stack of books and climbed to the room she shared with Rosalie.

"There you are." Rosalie grasped Mia's hands and all

but dragged her to the dressing table. "Sit. I will do your hair."

Mia balked. "Don't you want to take the time to make yourself prettier?"

"I can do my own hair in a trice. Now sit." She pushed on Mia's shoulders.

Mia sat. The woman who faced her in the mirror looked pale and tired with shadows beneath her eyes and puffiness around them. "It'll take more than a new hairstyle to make me look better."

"Oh, that's right. Ma sent this up." Rosalie darted across the room, dipped a folded cloth in the ewer, then sprinkled a few drops of oil onto it. The scent of lavender swirled through the room. "Hold this to your eyes."

Mia took the cloth and laid it across her eyelids. For a second it burned, then the soothing essence started its magic and tension began to drain from her neck and shoulders. Rosalie's ministrations with the hairbrush added its effect to her well-being. So did the silence in the room. For once, Rosalie chose not to speak but focused on her work, brushing, twisting and pinning with deft fingers.

During the quarter hour of silence Mia could do nothing but think or pray. The former she rarely did beyond what was necessary for her work. The latter she did too infrequently.

Once upon a time, she had spent no less than a half hour a day on her knees, usually more.

*Did I leave You behind, as well, Lord?*

Thinking back, the last time Mia recalled praying for any length of time was before she left Hillsdale. Once gone, executing the articles she had been hired to write and too busy finding her new way and more work in the city, she had abandoned her communion with the Lord. She had read her Bible and gone to church most Sundays, but she hadn't spent time on her knees talking to Jesus or, more important, listening for Him.

She listened for him then, her soul aching, her heart battered. She heard nothing. *Lord,* she cried out in silence, *I don't know what to do. I love Ayden, but he's determined to stay here and do whatever he must to do so.*

No word came to Mia except Rosalie's muttered, "Oops."

Mia started to remove the cloth from her eyes.

Rosalie laid a staying hand over Mia's. "Don't look. Trust me. You'll be beautiful when I'm done."

Mia smiled and kept her eyes closed. If the cold water and lavender lessened the redness of her eyes before anyone else saw her, the stillness was worth the trouble.

*I can't stay here, Lord. I have nowhere to live and not enough in savings to get me through until I find other work, unless I sell this story of Jamie's abduction. I could have a permanent, steady position back in Boston.*

Rosalie gave out a low cry of delight. "This is stunning, if I may say so myself. But don't look. We'll get you dressed first."

In another quarter hour, Rosalie allowed Mia to look in the dressing table mirror. A stranger looked back at her, a lady who had taken time and care with her appearance, from the crown of curls atop her head, to the pearl drops suspended from her earlobes, to the flowered blue silk dress with its tiers billowing over wide hoops and topped with a jacket in the same color.

"This is too formal for a dinner with the family," Mia said.

"No, it's not." Rosalie began attending to her own dark curls. "Trust me."

Mia narrowed her eyes. "That's the third time you've

said that. It's making me think I shouldn't trust you. Do you have something up your sleeve?"

Rosalie giggled. "Not me. I never—"

She broke off at the sound of the doorbell. "That'll be Fletcher, and here I am not dressed yet. Will you go down and entertain him until I'm ready?"

"Of course." She might be able to finagle some information about the baby out of the deputy.

But when she got downstairs, she found Mr. Goswell and Mr. Divine with Fletcher Lambert. Ayden likely was still with Charmaine.

Mia felt sick. If the trains had been running, she would have gotten on the next one out of town, even if it were going west.

But she couldn't leave until the next day. The men rose at her entrance, and Mr. Divine came forward to take her hand in both of his. "I'm glad to see you looking better, Miss Roper. Did you have a productive afternoon?"

"For the past hour I did manage to work, thank you. Did Miss Judd finish her assignment? She seemed frustrated."

"I expect she will get it done all right." Mr. Divine's smile grew warm enough to embarrass Mia. "She's a determined lady. Would you like to join us?"

"I should help Mrs. Goswell."

"Ayden was helping her," Mr. Goswell said. "Now he's in the sitting room reading your articles. They were left out, so I thought you might not mind."

"I said he could read the one on the college women and the wreck. They're—" Mia halted and compressed her lips.

She hadn't said he could read the one on Jamie's abduction. He hadn't liked the idea of her writing it, and she had left it on the secretary along with the others. She needed to retrieve it before it was too late.

"Will you all excuse me?" She spun on one heel, sending her hoops rocking, and raced from the room.

She nearly ran into Mrs. Goswell coming out of the sitting room, her lips closed but curved up at the corners as though she were up to mischief.

The smile broadened when she saw Mia. "Just in time. Go on in."

"Just in time for what?"

Mrs. Goswell didn't answer. She simply opened the sitting room door without turning around, then retreated to the kitchen.

Mia stood on the threshold with parted lips and widening eyes. She ran her hand across her brow, then lowered it to the same scene, an intimate romantic scene. A small table had been covered in a white linen cloth and laid for two with crystal candlesticks in the middle holding long, white tapers. Beyond the table, Ayden stood at the tall desk, her papers spread out before him, his shoulders stiff enough to balance the flickering candles without danger of knocking them to the ground.

"Shut the door. You're letting in the cold air." That melodious voice that usually caressed her ears with its warmth sounded frostier than the air from outside icing the windows.

Mia shut the door. Her hoop stopped her from leaning against it, but she stood as erect as a schoolgirl about to receive a lecture for bad behavior. She crossed her arms over her front. "You found it."

"It's not like you hid it." Ayden faced her, his blue eyes nearly black in the candlelight, his mouth grim. "Why do you need to write it?"

"It's money in the bank, and I need all of that I can get."

"Are you so poor?" His gaze swept her blue silk gown.

"I'm a good steward of my money."

"Just not others' privacy."

"It won't hurt anyone if I write that article."

"Won't it?" His palm slapped the papers. "It will further disrupt that child's life to have strangers swarm around him. It will endanger him further if others learn his family is wealthy enough to make kidnapping worth the risk. It will give others ideas of doing the same to other children."

"Don't be naive, Ayden." Mia moved toward him with the intent of taking her partially written article out of his reach. "People come up with ideas of crime on their own."

"Or is it articles like this that give them even more notions?"

"I write about incidents after they happen, after the criminal has acted—not before."

"And if you didn't report on it, would so much of it continue? Don't you think as a lady and a Christian you should stay with articles that uplift and encourage?"

Mia rocked back on her heels as though punched in the solar plexus. "How dare you tell me how to do my job? I don't tell you how to teach."

"Of course you may do your job as you see fit." He sighed and rolled his shoulders. "But you said you wouldn't write this."

"I said I would think about it." She waved her hand toward the table. "And right now we need to think of how to get out of this cozy little dinner for two."

"I intend on handling it by eating it. I'm starving." He crossed to the table and drew out a chair. "We'll have less fuss if we just give in."

"What about Miss Finney? Won't she care that you're eating dinner with me?"

Ayden shrugged. "You're an old family friend now, nothing more."

Mia flinched. "You can dismiss your past commitment

to me so easily?" Suddenly, she could scarcely breathe. She could scarcely see. "It meant so little to you?"

"It meant everything to me."

"Except for the part about you not coming with me." Mia closed the distance between them, the firmness of her strides sending her skirts swaying and swishing like windtossed treetops. "So what happens to your commitment to Miss Finney if her father can't persuade the others to hire you permanently? Do you abandon her like you did me?"

"*You* abandoned *me*. You made a promise—"

"Don't you talk to me about promises. *You* made a promise to *me*." She jabbed her finger into the center of his chest. "You said you'd love me forever." She poked him again. "You said you would honor and respect my wish to write. You—"

He clasped her jabbing finger in his hand. "I had no future in Boston. You wouldn't listen to me about that. You wanted your own way without listening to my side of things. And now, Mia, *mi amore*…" He closed his eyes and raised her hand to his cheek.

The motion drew her forward. Her other hand grasped his shoulder for balance. He wrapped his free arm around her waist, and she was in his arms, her hands clinging to his shoulders, her lips clinging to his.

He kissed her like a starving man took nourishment—deeply, thoroughly, as though breath itself took second place to the cherished contact of the embrace.

Mia slid her fingers into the thick, soft waves of his hair and yearned for the kiss to never stop. But a closing door, a giggle and the need to breathe intruded.

Ayden released Mia first. He yanked his hands from her waist and shoved them into his pockets as though her cool silk had turned to hot coals. "I'm sorry. I had no right to do that."

She gave him a tentative smile. "I didn't stop you."

"But you should have." Ayden fisted his hand around his somewhat crumpled neck cloth. "I should have stopped it before it started. We have no right to behave this way." He began to pace from door to table. "We're not engaged anymore. And we won't be again. Your future is in Boston and mine is here."

Mia clasped her hands at her throat to hide her racing pulse. "It's not if you break things off with Miss Finney."

"Which means I have no future at all. I don't have any job prospects elsewhere."

"You could get them."

Ayden turned on her, his palms up as though warding off a blow. "When you give up your position in the East?"

Mia bit her lower lip.

Ayden smiled without humor. "I didn't think so. You aren't willing to go with me wherever I can find work because you might not be able to be a lady of letters wherever that is, or so you think."

"Or fear," Mia whispered.

"And I fear not being able to find work."

"So you'll still offer for Miss Finney just to have a job?"

"And a wife who is a helpmeet, not a competitor to see which of us can succeed faster." He stalked from the room, and a moment later, the front door slammed.

The cry of protest she would not utter choking her, Mia snatched up her story of Jamie's kidnapping, tore it in half and threw it in the fire.

## Chapter 14

Ayden started walking. His footfalls crunched on the frozen snow, loud in the quiet of the night. By the light of moonlight and starlight and lamps glowing in people's houses reflecting off of the whiteness, he paced through the streets to the campus then beyond. His lungs ached from the cold. His heart ached from the love he had abandoned. His conscience ached from the actions he had taken.

Worse, his conscience ached from the action he had intended to make.

"What was I thinking, Lord?" Alone in the countryside, he cried aloud.

He was thinking that, with Mia out of his life, as he thought, for good, marrying a woman for whom he had respect and admiration was good enough. Even without the benefit of being wed to the daughter of the director of his department, he would have made Charmaine an offer. He needed a wife and a home of his own. It was time to join the ranks of his sober and respectable colleagues. Single men were always a problem in the social gatherings he was expected to attend. The hostesses needed to find an acceptable female to even out the numbers. Charmaine already belonged in those ranks, accepted by professor's wives as her father's hostess. So she was a logical choice for a wife.

But Mia owned Ayden's heart, and she was not gone forever. She still loved him. She hadn't said it, but her kiss told him she did.

"But she doesn't love me enough to stay." Ayden leaned against an oak and covered his face with his hands. Without gloves, his fingers were numb. If only his heart had remained as frozen as his extremities. "She will leave me to make her fame and fortune with that story about the abducted child. She loves her work more than she loves me."

But didn't he love his work more than her a year and a half earlier—and now? He had compared the position in Boston and the one offered him in Hillsdale and saw more of a future in his hometown with his family and friends around him, people who wouldn't mock him for his faith or expect him to behave in ways that countered his moral and spiritual convictions, as they too often had during his years as a student. They had respected and been impressed enough with his academic acumen to want him to pass his knowledge on to others, but they had never understood the life he chose outside the college campus. At home, he got both, with the love of his parents and sister close at hand and that of his brother and his family on their frequent visits home.

"How can I give that up, Lord?"

How could he not for the woman he loved?

Certain he would transform into one of Rosalie's snowmen if he didn't get moving, he turned his footsteps toward town. He didn't go home. He veered his course to a house too large for the number of inhabitants and pulled the cord for the doorbell with perhaps more vigor than necessary.

From beyond the oval glass pane in the door rumbled the murmur of voices rising and falling in polite dialogue.

Ayden rang the bell again.

The murmur of voices continued. Footfalls clicking on hardwood floors added a staccato beat to the rumble. Then Dr. Finney stood in the doorway.

"I need to see Charmaine." Ayden made his request before the older man could speak.

Finney scowled. "She is waiting on my guests. You are scheduled to attend her tomorrow."

"I need to see her tonight." Ayden's voice shook just a little.

Finney scanned him from his head without a hat, to his lack of an overcoat, to his hands without gloves. His mouth thinned, but he stepped back so Ayden could pass him and enter the house.

Even the unheated entryway felt warm compared to the outside temperature.

"She's in the kitchen preparing coffee for my guests." Finney's face softened. "Go get yourself warm." Already stooped shoulders slumping, head bowed, he returned to the parlor.

Feet dragging, Ayden rounded the graceful curve of the stairway and entered the kitchen. Charmaine stood at the table arranging china cups on a silver tray. She glanced up at his entrance, and a cup slipped from her fingers.

Ayden dove forward and caught it before it hit the stone floor. "I'm sorry to startle you." He set the delicate china on its saucer. "I had to talk to you."

"I know." She sank onto one of the chairs and folded her arms atop the table. "I heard about your fencing bout this morning. I heard about the sledding accident yesterday. I saw how you kept looking toward the door this afternoon." Her face resembled that of a painted china doll—beautiful and devoid of emotion. But whether she looked blank because she loved him and the hurt ran too deep to show or because she simply didn't care enough, Ayden doubted he would ever know.

That made him sadder than if she had wept and wailed and clung to him.

He crouched down beside her. "I never should have courted you. I knew, deep in my heart, I still loved her. I simply covered it up with ambition and my deep fondness and respect for you. If she'd never come back…"

"We would have had a perfectly comfortable and boring life together."

"I don't think that at all. Believe me, Charmaine, you are—"

"Don't say it." She held up one hand, palm toward him. Her nose wrinkled. "I am a beautiful woman who will find someone who loves me one day because I'm intelligent and kind and worthy and all that rot." Her lower lip quivered ever so slightly and the pale blue of her eyes brightened. "You know, Ayden Goswell, I've heard that speech before."

Ayden rocked back on his heels, his eyes widening.

Charmaine emitted a ladylike bark of laughter. "You look shocked. Do you think you were the first man who's courted me with an eye to marriage? I am nearly twenty-three."

"Of course not, but I can't believe he let you go."

"You're letting me go."

"I discovered I still love another lady. Surely…" He rose to slide more wood into the stove.

"Surely he didn't leave me for the same reason? No, he loved me. His name was Dermott Druggett. He had eyes as blue as yours but hair the color of a raven. He was ten times richer than Daddy, but because he spoke with an Irish accent and grew up on the streets of Dublin, Daddy didn't approve. So Dermott tried to convince me he didn't love me enough to wed me, just enough to let me go free."

Ayden slammed the lid onto the wood box. "He was a fool not to simply drag you away."

"Or maybe I was the fool to let him go." Charmaine rose and pulled the coffeepot from the stove. "Will she stay here?"

"She has a position back in Boston, and I am likely not to have one here for long. But, if she'll have me, I'll go and muck out stables until I find teaching work, if I must."

"I'm not supposed to tell you this, but you are going to be offered the permanent position at the college. They are going to notify the other candidates and you tomorrow."

Ayden's heart leaped, then raced until it stumbled and twisted over knowing what he was giving up. What he must give up. "I'll still go to her."

"I want to be loved like that." Charmaine blinked back tears.

Ayden took her hands in his. "I think you were. He let you go so you didn't have to choose between loyalty to your father and loyalty to him."

"Then I wasn't the one who didn't love him enough to make the choice for him." She rose on tiptoe and kissed his cheek. "I wish Miss Roper would choose to stay here with you. This is a fine place to raise a family. I much prefer it to the city. But I think perhaps it's time I went back."

"To him?"

"If he'll have me."

"He will." He embraced her as a friend, a lady of character who he suddenly liked more than he had throughout their courtship. Then he quietly left the house. On his way home, he said a prayer for Charmaine to have the strength to go after the man she still loved, a man about whom she had told him nothing, likely for the same reason Ayden had told her nothing of his feelings for Mia. They wanted the same things—security, family, a position of respect and purpose in the community. Marriage to one another would have given them both that. They would have had everything but the people they truly loved.

A little light-headed over the enormous error they had both come too close to making in the name of ambition and convenience, Ayden slipped through the back door of his house and into the kitchen, the only room where a light still burned.

His parents sat at the table drinking tea and holding hands. Thirty-five years of marriage and they still held hands across a table.

They glanced up at his entrance and smiled below raised eyebrows.

"You look cold," Ma observed. "Are you trying to catch lung fever going out without a hat, gloves or overcoat?"

"I didn't think about the cold. I didn't think at all. I just had to get away."

"Why?" Pa's dark blue eyes pinned Ayden to the center of the floor. "What did you say to her?"

"Or she to you?" Ma added.

Despite the chill still racing through him, Ayden's face heated and he tried to look away. "It's not what either of us said. It's, um..." He shifted from foot to foot like a child commanded to confess slipping a garter snake into Rosalie's bed, knowing the consequences would prove uncomfortable. "I kissed her."

"Then I presume you intend to marry her." Pa made a statement; he didn't ask a question.

Ayden nodded. "If she'll have me."

"Will you move to Boston?" Ma asked.

"At the end of this quarter, yes. Tomorrow morning, I'll withdraw my application for the permanent position."

"What will you do to support her in the city?" Pa asked.

Ayden smiled. "Euphemia Roper is perfectly capable of supporting herself. And I'll find work. Maybe not teaching at first, but I'll find something. That doesn't matter if I'm with her. And…and…" He faltered. "And she wants me there with her." He took a step back to the door. "Is she upstairs? I'd like to tell her…ask her…"

Pa shook his head. "Not tonight. I think, because of what you did to her in the past, you need to withdraw your application first and then make her an offer."

Ayden opened his mouth to protest but saw the wisdom of his father's counsel and inclined his head. "I'll be on campus first thing in the morning."

His parents' faces shone with pride and love as they wished him good-night. Leaving them would hurt, but the Bible did say that a man would leave his mother. He should have acted on that verse before. He should have taken their wisdom before. He should have asked the Lord what He wanted for his life instead of going his own way.

Certain he wouldn't sleep, Ayden went into the sitting room to write the letter withdrawing his application for the professorship at the college. A few embers glowed on the hearth. As he started to add kindling to replenish the flames, he noticed a scrap of paper singed on one edge but not consumed. He plucked it out and read what words showed on the torn bit of paper.

*Ransom note fo—*

Two full and one partial word were all Ayden needed to see to realize she had burned her story about the abducted child.

"It could just be a draft." He sprinted for the desk.

Her other two articles lay in neat stacks held down by

books. Nowhere did he find a single word about the abduction.

"Oh, Mia, *mi amore.*" He clung to the secretary as if
it were an anchor keeping him from sailing up the stairs
and pounding on Rosalie's door.

His parents were right. He needed to sever his ties to
Hillsdale completely before he could go to Mia offering
her a heart unfettered to anything but hers.

He drew out paper, pen and ink and began to write his
letter of resignation.

# *Chapter 15*

In ten minutes, the first train in over a week was scheduled to pull into Hillsdale, the town Mia Roper hoped to call home once again. Whether or not she had calculated correctly and that home would be with Ayden Goswell, she didn't know. He had come home after she was in bed and left before she rose without leaving her a message. Nonetheless, she bundled up in her warm clothes, tucked her purse and portfolio under her arm and headed for the train depot in town.

The station resembled a lemonade stand during a Fourth of July celebration. Lines snaked out the door and around the corner. Voices rose and fell in animated dialogue, and children wove through the crowd in a game of tag, their clear voices piercing the frosty air like bells. Even waiting in the cold, people smiled and chattered, their faces bright and hopeful.

"Those with eastbound tickets for today get on first," a

railroad worker shouted from the depot doorway. "Tickets for today. Right now, we have no more seats on this incoming eastbound train."

Many faces fell. A few groans rose into the crystal sky.

"Westbound?" some shouted.

The conductor leaned back into the depot, then stepped outside again. "Westbound train has a few seats available. First come, first served."

"Ma, we'll never get there in time," an adolescent boy protested.

"I'm just believing Jesus will provide," announced a woman with a baby in her arms.

A chorus of "Amen" swelled through the crowd.

Mia started past the line, headed for the station doorway. If she could get her money back for her ticket, she would have more than enough to support her until she sold her articles and got paid for them. She could probably charge more than the ticket cost.

Mrs. Goswell had offered her room in their house for as long as Mia wanted to stay. "We have the space now that Mr. Divine is leaving us."

But if Ayden ended up offering Charmaine marriage, Mia didn't want to meet him over the breakfast table.

Heart pounding, she explained to the conductor at the door that she had a ticket to exchange and a telegram to send. He waved her inside to the ticket counter. A rotund man with white hair standing on end in the hot, dry air was examining tickets and waving people through the door to the platform with the rapidity of a steam shuttle.

"Next," he barked to the line before him. "People are waiting. Have your ticket ready."

Mia joined the line and drew forth her ticket. When her turn came, she laid it on the counter. "I would like to redeem this ticket. I am not returning to Boston at this time."

Without looking at her, the agent picked up the ticket, glanced at it, then handed it back to her. "You'll get more money for it if you sell it outside."

"But I—" Mia blinked.

More money meant she could leave the Goswells sooner rather than later—just in case…

She retrieved her ticket, then crossed to the telegraph office. Her message was brief.

*Not returning. Stop. Sending two articles. Stop.*

With the secure future she craved from childhood sent flying with that telegram, Mia headed back out the door. More passengers filed into the station.

"Eastbound train is filled," the ticket agent shouted.

"When's the next train?" several people chorused.

"Eastbound tonight," the conductor answered. "Twelve hours."

The holiday mood subsided.

"There's a little lady here willing to sell hers." The ticket agent pointed at Mia hovering in the doorway.

A sea of hopeful faces turned toward Mia. She clutched her purse more closely for fear someone would snatch it with the precious ticket.

Gold and silver flashed before her eyes along with shouts of offers to buy. She scanned the crowd to see who most needed the ticket. Her gaze fell on the woman with the infant.

She shook her head. "I only have the cost of the ticket, nothing extra. But don't worry about me. The Lord will provide."

The sums shoved in Mia's face tempted her. Those coins signified independence and security for weeks.

She ducked beneath the arm of a gentleman in a silk hat and walked up to the woman. "Take it and God bless."

The woman's eyes glowed. "You're certain? You can get so much more from others."

"Keep your coin. Get you and your baby home."

"Thank you." The woman started to cry. "My husband hasn't seen our baby yet. Bless you. Thank you."

Mia gave her a nudge. "Get on that platform before the train arrives."

Heart warm and calm for the first time in eighteen months, Mia watched the woman until she vanished into the station, then she took a step back out of the throng and into something hard pressed to her spine.

"Say nothing and no one'll get hurt," a male voice rasped in her ear.

A chill deeper than the cold air could reach ran through Mia. "What do you want from me?"

"What do you think? The child."

Ayden's heart raced with anticipation, with apprehension, with exertion from his jog from campus to home in order to see Mia as quickly as possible. But when he reached the house, Rosalie was home alone.

"She left for the train station more than an hour ago," Rosalie said.

"The train?" A lump swelled in Ayden's chest. "She left? I thought… I was certain…"

He had just destroyed his future for a lady who still found her career more important than he was.

Rosalie giggled and kissed his cheek. "Don't look so woebegone, brother. She didn't leave Hillsdale. She went there to turn in her ticket. Of course, I did expect her back sooner than this. Maybe she changed her mind."

"I'll change my mind about Lambert if you're not careful." Ayden tugged on one of Rosalie's curls, causing the left side of her coiffeur to tumble onto her shoulder.

"Oh, you." She gave him a playful slap on his hand but sobered at once. "Seriously, Ayden, she should have come home by now. She didn't take her things with her except for her notebook and purse, and if she was just going to turn in her—"

Her voice died behind him as he slammed out the kitchen door.

He reached the station in minutes and began searching the crowd for signs of Mia. He spied many mothers, wives, daughters trying to get passage on one of the trains finally able to get down the tracks. But no sign of Mia.

After a quarter hour, he managed to reach the ticket counter. "Did you see a pretty young woman come by here?" At the man's blank look, he clarified, "Chestnut hair. Green eyes. A hood with white fur."

"'Bout an hour ago. The ticket clerk tapped his chin. "She wanted to get a refund for her ticket. I suggested she sell it. Get more money."

Ayden's heart leaped. "Did she?"

"Nope. She gave it away."

She gave away her ticket. She was staying.

Ayden would have run through the streets singing about what a blessed man he was—if only he knew where Mia had gone.

"Did you see—"

"Look, mister, I have a hundred people to get out of here. I can't keep track of one foolish female."

"Of course not. Thank you for your help."

Ayden left the station. Perhaps she had gone to Genevieve's or the boardinghouse or even the church. Or she might have gone to the sheriff for information on the child.

But no, she had tossed that article into the fire.

Those who knew about her telegrams wouldn't know

that. They might think she had visited the station to pass along or gather more information.

His guts coiling like a snake ready to spring, Ayden ran to Genevieve's house. Only the merest hint of smoke puffed from the kitchen chimney, and no one answered his knock. Likewise, the church, for the first time in a week, lay quiet and empty.

Footfalls slowing, Ayden made his way toward the sheriff's office. He saw a few acquaintances along the way and asked about Mia. None had seen her. Mouth dry and temples beginning to throb, Ayden entered the sheriff's office.

For once, he was glad to see Fletcher Lambert on duty.

"How may I help you?" Lambert, now his future brother-in-law, grinned and raised a hand in greeting.

"Mia is missing." Ayden grasped the edge of the counter. "She went to the train station to turn in her ticket, and no one has seen her since."

"You're sure?" Lambert leaned forward, his eyes growing dark. "She's not—"

"Anywhere unless she's gotten home in the past quarter hour or so."

"Let's go see." Lambert stepped into the back office for a moment, then returned, pulling on his overcoat. "Sheriff says I can go with you. All the others are guarding the station." He lowered his voice though the office was empty. "We sent the child home this morning, but the kidnappers are still at large and aren't likely to know we no longer have the boy here."

The child. The kidnappers. They would surely not bother with Mia. She knew nothing.

But she had sent those telegrams, so the kidnappers might think she did.

Ayden and Lambert sprinted for the Goswell house.

Halfway there, they met Rosalie racing through the slush. She was waving a sheet of paper and screaming.

A gun pressing into her ribs prodding her forward in silence, Mia stumbled through the trees and into an overgrown but still familiar yard. She knew the yard, the back of the house, the kitchen into which the false railroad worker shoved her.

Through her own blurred vision and a pall of smoke from a charcoal brazier in the middle of the stone floor, she peered at the table where she had often helped prepare lemonade and sweets to feed hungry college students, the stove where she had set many a pot of coffee to brew. The stove lay cold and the table served as a bed for a woman with one leg splinted and swathed in bandages. Nothing else in the chamber was the same as the last time she had visited Professor and Mrs. Blamey. Black cloth instead of frilly gingham covered the windows. Candles flickered in saucer holders atop the stove and on shelves meant for dishes. The only warmth radiated from the brazier, pitiful at best and of little use in a frigid Michigan February.

Shivering uncontrollably, her mouth dry, Mia fixed her attention on the woman and tried to speak in a voice that gave away nothing of her desire to scream. "You've been holed up here all along? We intended to help you."

"I crawled out the back of the car the minute I realized you had the Yardley brat." The woman's voice was tight. Lines of pain etched her face. "If my leg wasn't broken already, it was broken after I landed on the ground, you interfering—"

"Enough talking." The gunman closed the door and shoved Mia forward. "Where are the others?"

"Sleeping in the dining room." The woman closed her eyes and fumbled a flat, green bottle to her lips. The stench of spirits and something else filled the room along with the smoke. Laudanum. The woman must be in terrible pain.

Mia hugged her arms over her middle. "Help me and we can get you proper medical care."

"Tabard here has done well enough." The woman closed her eyes. "Just give us the baby and we can get all the money we need for all the doctors in the world."

"I don't know where he is." Mia doubted the woman would believe her any more than her abductor had. "I don't know. I don't know. I don't—" She heard the rising note in her voice and clamped her lips together.

Tabard nudged her with the gun. "Turn around. Agnes, tie her hands."

Shaking, Mia kept her hands tucked beneath her arms.

"Put your hands behind you." Tabard shoved the gun harder into Mia's ribs.

Mia put her hands behind her. "You won't get anywhere with this. I don't know where Jamie is."

"Goswell does." Agnes began to wind rough hemp around Mia's wrists.

Her heart crawled into her throat, threatening to strangle her. "They won't sacrifice the baby for me. I won't l-let them."

Could she burn through her bonds with the brazier? She risked firing her clothes and blistering her skin, but—

"We don't want to harm the baby. We just want money for him." Tabard handed his gun to Agnes and crouched to tie Mia's ankles. "But you are worth nothing, so we *will* harm you."

She opened her mouth to dispute his claim of no harm to the baby, then closed her lips. If she remained silent, perhaps they wouldn't gag her.

"Keep holding her," Tabard said. "I'm fetching the others."

Two men with more guns trooped into the kitchen and arranged themselves near the door and window. Mia sat on the floor beneath the table and concentrated on not being sick. She must free herself and alert the sheriff to warn whomever had the baby.

Black spots danced before her eyes. Her head filled with mush and muddled thoughts. Must. Get. Away. Must. Warn. Must—

The two men looking outside leaped back from the window and door. "They're here," Tabard announced. "I knew Goswell wouldn't risk the girl's life." He caressed the barrel of his gun, then turned the muzzle on Mia.

"You were the man on the railway car." A surge of energy pulsed through her, and she shot out her bound feet, striking him across the ankles.

Tabard swore and pulled the trigger.

Mia rolled beneath the table, kicking at the legs, a chair, the brazier. Agnes screamed. The men shouted. Another gun blast roared through the room.

The inside kitchen door burst open.

Through a tangle of hair and the rungs of a chair, Mia stared at Ayden Goswell and the bundle in his arms. "You think you can trade my lady for this child," Ayden shouted, "then take him."

And he threw the child straight at Tabard.

Tabard dropped his weapon and grabbed for the baby. A second man charged for Ayden, gun raised. Mia kicked a chair into his path. He crashed to the floor, his bullet blasting away plaster from the ceiling.

Diving beneath the table, Ayden cleared the way for Lambert and two other deputies, guns drawn, to swarm into the kitchen and secure the kidnappers. Two of the men charged for the back door. Lambert brought one down with a shot to his leg. The other tripped over the swaddled bundle and lost his weapon. Before he retrieved it, a deputy held him at the muzzle of his weapon.

Tabard remained motionless, his mouth open, his eyes wide and staring at the baby head he held in his hands.

"It's a doll." Mia started to giggle. "It's one of Rosalie's dolls."

"My mother never throws anything away." Ayden slid out from beneath the table and drew Mia after him. "Let me get you untied."

He produced a knife no longer than an index finger and looking as old as ancient Rome and sliced through Mia's bonds. Then, while the deputies shuffled the three criminals and Agnes out of the house, Ayden held Mia close, kissing her brow, her eyes and, finally, her lips. "I love you, Mia, *mi amore*. I never stopped. I was a fool to think I could live without you, even here. I won't again. I'll come to Boston or Philadelphia or Bombay as long as—"

"Shh." She laid a finger over his lips. "No need. I sent a telegram to tell my editor I won't be coming back."

"Mia." He held her at arm's length, then released her shoulders to take her hand and draw her into the clean, crisp air of the overgrown garden. "Too smoky in there. I couldn't see your beautiful eyes. Did you say you aren't returning to Boston?"

"I'll have my things sent to me here."

"But what will you do for work?"

"I can write some articles from here and tutor and teach fencing and…" She gave him a coy smile. "Perhaps find a great deal more to occupy my time."

Ayden rubbed the back of his neck and took several quick breaths. "Like being my wife? We needn't stay here. I turned in my letter of resignation so I could go with you."

"Oh, Ayden." Mia lost her battle with tears, rested her head against his broad shoulder and wept. "I don't want to

go back to Boston. I want to stay here where I am loved."
She raised her head. "I never stopped loving you, either.
I didn't ask for this assignment, but apparently the Lord
had other plans for me. But what—" She toyed with the
top button on his coat. "What about Charmaine?"

Ayden's smile was gentle, a little rueful. "Apparently
she left for the East on the first train out of town this morning. You see, there's a certain Irish businessman out there
she thinks is worth trying to remind he loved her once."

"Unless he's a fool, she'll succeed." Hand still shaking,
Mia stroked Ayden's cheek. "But what about your professorship? If you resigned, how can you stay here?"

"I don't know what Charmaine said to her father, but Dr.
Finney is…" Ayden shook his head. "Subdued this morning. I thought he might cry when I resigned."

"He thinks the world of you—that's obvious."

"He said if I change my mind about accepting the position, or you are as brilliant as he thinks you are and decide
to stay, I can reapply for the position. And if they decide
against me…" He shrugged. "I can work with Pa in the
hardware store or apply for work elsewhere—if you need
to go elsewhere to work. I just want to be with you."

"Change your mind about accepting the position?" Mia
took half a step back. "You mean they were going to offer
you the professorship after all?"

Ayden inclined his head. "Charmaine told me last night.
I wanted to make you an offer of marriage last night, but I
needed to be sure you knew I was free first." He curved his
hands around her cheeks and tilted her face up. "I needed
you to know that's how serious I am this time about how
much I love you and want you to marry me." He glanced
around him at the garden where he had first proposed on
a warm, moonlit night. He smiled. "Will you marry me,
Miss Roper? I love you with all my heart."

"And I love you with all my heart." She rose on tiptoe and kissed him. "I'll marry you and stay here or go anywhere, as long as I am with you, Professor Goswell."

\* \* \* \* \*

# REQUEST YOUR FREE BOOKS!

## 2 FREE INSPIRATIONAL NOVELS
## PLUS 2
## FREE
## MYSTERY GIFTS

*Love Inspired*

**YES!** Please send me 2 FREE Love Inspired® novels and my 2 FREE mystery gifts (gifts are worth about $10). After receiving them, if I don't wish to receive any more books, I can return the shipping statement marked "cancel." If I don't cancel, I will receive 6 brand-new novels every month and be billed just $4.74 per book in the U.S. or $5.24 per book in Canada. That's a savings of at least 21% off the cover price. It's quite a bargain! Shipping and handling is just 50¢ per book in the U.S. and 75¢ per book in Canada.* I understand that accepting the 2 free books and gifts places me under no obligation to buy anything. I can always return a shipment and cancel at any time. Even if I never buy another book, the two free books and gifts are mine to keep forever.

105/305 IDN F49N

Name _____ (PLEASE PRINT)

Address _____ Apt. #

City _____ State/Prov. _____ Zip/Postal Code

Signature (if under 18, a parent or guardian must sign)

### Mail to the **Harlequin® Reader Service:**
**IN U.S.A.:** P.O. Box 1867, Buffalo, NY 14240-1867
**IN CANADA:** P.O. Box 609, Fort Erie, Ontario L2A 5X3

**Are you a subscriber to Love Inspired books
and want to receive the larger-print edition?
Call 1-800-873-8635 or visit www.ReaderService.com.**

* Terms and prices subject to change without notice. Prices do not include applicable taxes. Sales tax applicable in N.Y. Canadian residents will be charged applicable taxes. Offer not valid in Quebec. This offer is limited to one order per household. Not valid for current subscribers to Love Inspired books. All orders subject to credit approval. Credit or debit balances in a customer's account(s) may be offset by any other outstanding balance owed by or to the customer. Please allow 4 to 6 weeks for delivery. Offer available while quantities last.

**Your Privacy**—The Harlequin® Reader Service is committed to protecting your privacy. Our Privacy Policy is available online at www.ReaderService.com or upon request from the Harlequin Reader Service.
We make a portion of our mailing list available to reputable third parties that offer products we believe may interest you. If you prefer that we not exchange your name with third parties, or if you wish to clarify or modify your communication preferences, please visit us at www.ReaderService.com/consumerschoice or write to us at Harlequin Reader Service Preference Service, P.O. Box 9062, Buffalo, NY 14269. Include your complete name and address.

LIDIR13R

# REQUEST YOUR FREE BOOKS!

## 2 FREE INSPIRATIONAL NOVELS
## PLUS 2
# FREE
## MYSTERY GIFTS

*Love Inspired.*
# HISTORICAL
### INSPIRATIONAL HISTORICAL ROMANCE

---

**YES!** Please send me 2 FREE Love Inspired® Historical novels and my 2 FREE mystery gifts (gifts are worth about $10). After receiving them, if I don't wish to receive any more books, I can return the shipping statement marked "cancel." If I don't cancel, I will receive 4 brand-new novels every month and be billed just $4.74 per book in the U.S. or $5.24 per book in Canada. That's a savings of at least 21% off the cover price. It's quite a bargain! Shipping and handling is just 50¢ per book in the U.S. and 75¢ per book in Canada.* I understand that accepting the 2 free books and gifts places me under no obligation to buy anything. I can always return a shipment and cancel at any time. Even if I never buy another book, the two free books and gifts are mine to keep forever.

102/302 IDN F5CY

| | | |
|---|---|---|
| Name | (PLEASE PRINT) | |
| Address | | Apt. # |
| City | State/Prov. | Zip/Postal Code |

Signature (if under 18, a parent or guardian must sign)

### Mail to the Harlequin® Reader Service:
**IN U.S.A.:** P.O. Box 1867, Buffalo, NY 14240-1867
**IN CANADA:** P.O. Box 609, Fort Erie, Ontario L2A 5X3

**Want to try two free books from another series?**
**Call 1-800-873-8635 or visit www.ReaderService.com.**

\* Terms and prices subject to change without notice. Prices do not include applicable taxes. Sales tax applicable in N.Y. Canadian residents will be charged applicable taxes. Offer not valid in Quebec. This offer is limited to one order per household. Not valid for current subscribers to Love Inspired Historical books. All orders subject to credit approval. Credit or debit balances in a customer's account(s) may be offset by any other outstanding balance owed by or to the customer. Please allow 4 to 6 weeks for delivery. Offer available while quantities last.

**Your Privacy**—The Harlequin® Reader Service is committed to protecting your privacy. Our Privacy Policy is available online at www.ReaderService.com or upon request from the Harlequin Reader Service.

We make a portion of our mailing list available to reputable third parties that offer products we believe may interest you. If you prefer that we not exchange your name with third parties, or if you wish to clarify or modify your communication preferences, please visit us at www.ReaderService.com/consumerschoice or write to us at Harlequin Reader Service Preference Service, P.O. Box 9062, Buffalo, NY 14269. Include your complete name and address.

LIHDIR13R

# *ReaderService*.com

## Manage your account online!

- Review your order history
- Manage your payments
- Update your address

---

*We've designed
the Harlequin® Reader Service
website just for you.*

---

## Enjoy all the features!

- Reader excerpts from any series
- Respond to mailings and
  special monthly offers
- Discover new series available to you
- Browse the Bonus Bucks catalog
- Share your feedback

*Visit us at:*

**ReaderService.com**